THE WESTERN RAIDER:
THE GUN-PRAYER OF SILVER TRENT
AND OTHER STORIES

THE GUN-PRAYER
OF SILVER TRENT
AND OTHER STORIES

By Stone Cody

STEEGER BOOKS • 2021

PUBLISHING HISTORY

"The Gun-Prayer of Silver Trent" originally appeared in the September 1940 (Vol. 21, No. 4) issue of *Star Western* magazine. Copyright © 1940 by Popular Publications, Inc. Copyright renewed © 1967 and assigned to Steeger Properties, LLC. All rights reserved.

"The Secret of Torture Ranch" originally appeared in the December 1940 (Vol. 22, No. 3) issue of *Star Western* magazine. Copyright © 1940 by Popular Publications, Inc. Copyright renewed © 1967 and assigned to Steeger Properties, LLC. All rights reserved.

"One Last Raid For Trent's Hell-Hawks!" originally appeared in the February 1941 (Vol. 23, No. 1) issue of *Star Western* magazine. Copyright © 1941 by Popular Publications, Inc. Copyright renewed © 1968 and assigned to Steeger Properties, LLC. All rights reserved.

THE GUN-PRAYER
OF SILVER TRENT

T HE HORSE was a half-broken mustang which the girl would not have been riding, except that the corral had been emptied of most of its horses. He lifted up his head and snorted at the column of trotting steers that burst over the ridge ahead.

The faint sound of gunfire, getting louder, sounded behind the ridge. A lead steer bellowed, the sound like a trumpet rising to hysteria, and increased his pace to a run. One of the two men riding point spurred ahead and slapped his Stetson in the steer's face. Maria Odlum could hear him cursing in the clear still afternoon air.

Absorbed, she sat watching the scene, the tender curves of her mouth making a severe line, and her blue eyes narrowed. But her mind did not quite take all this in. It meant trouble, and just of what sort she did not know.

She had never looked at a scene like it, and because of it, this country of hers sprang out into sudden, sharp relief as though the tumbled iron hillsides had suddenly become alien and unfamiliar by the strangeness of this invasion.

A roadrunner darted out of the brush ahead of the oncoming steers, wings half lifted, running his long-legged, flashing race ahead of the steers, for the sheer fun of it.

Beneath her, the mustang stood trembling, then swung side-

ways, half rearing, wanting to go back. His snort was a quivering warning to which she paid no attention, absorbed in the scene before her.

The horse tried again to turn and when her sharp hand on the reins swung him back, he began to buck. It caught her off guard and nearly unseated her, but after a second she caught her balance and rode him, the instinctive balance of her body compensating for the surprise her mind felt. She had thought she had taken what mild buck there was in him out of him

2

The four vaqueros had stabbed for their guns and were coming up
now, blasting bullets at Silver and the pock-marked man....

when she had climbed into the saddle at the corral, but this was
something else again.

The mustang jolted savagely, stiff-legged, sunfished and then
changed ends like a shoo-fly reversing its flight. Maria had the
sudden salt taste of blood in her mouth as the jolts whipped her
spine and snapped her head back and front.

She had sudden desperate wonder as to whether or not she
could ride this one, and as sudden and desperate a sense of the
iron ground which the bucker's shod hoofs pounded—ground

which her body would hit as soft metal hits an anvil. Dazed, she held on and rode.

The mustang bucked sideways, slamming into a high, upstanding thrust of rock. Her lifted leg missed the impact, but the bucker's hind quarters slammed it so hard that he was nearly thrown.

He screamed in fury and jumped stiff-legged into a sunfish that had her left stirrup scraping ground. Even then it did not occur to her that he was bucking blind. She was too shaken and hammered to realize anything except that she must hang on.

The mustang quit bucking suddenly and jumped into a dead run. His course crossed that of the oncoming herd but missed the lead steers by a quarter of a hundred yards. The roadrunner, attacked from the flank, let out a queer, twanging squawk and swerved into brush.

The horse was headed toward the sharply dropping bank of an arroyo which she should have known but had forgotten in her half-dazed state. Even if she had realized she would have thought that the bronc would turn before he hit it, because it had not yet come to her that this was one of those rare animals who buck blind and stampede blind, oblivious of anything about them.

Behind her and to her left a voice yelled urgently, "Quit him! Quit him pronto! Swing your feet forward as you land."

THE WORDS made only a blurred impression and did nothing to change the set determination she had to sit this ride out, no matter what. Vaguely, she had the impression that the words had come from the other point rider—the one who had not cursed and slapped at the stampeding steer. But that didn't matter. She was too busy to listen. Her arms were straining at the reins, her jolted gaze fixed between the mustang's flattened ears.

Before her, the fifty foot drop of the arroyo ran like a wide knife slash from the slope of the ridge. Savagely, her knees clutched tight and her body jolted, she hung to the reins, sawing at them with all her waning strength.

The arroyo's edge loomed. The mustang squealed, blind with rage, racing toward that margin of death. Then something keened in the air over Maria's head, settled in a silken whisper over her.

Her taut arms whipped inward, burning. Something hard and relentless yet somehow gentle cut across her stomach. It came to her in a flash of rage that this thing was a rope.

Her hips hit the cantle of the saddle, hesitated and pulled over it as her feet came out of the stirrups. Briefly, she felt the bump of the mustang's sharp-boned hindquarters, and then she was sitting on air with the cruel cut of the rope inexorable about her stomach. Her feet hit the ground as the horse hurtled over the edge of the arroyo, feet flailing, a queer note of triumph in the vicious squeal that ripped his throat as he felt the weight lifted from his back and knew his body sailing into free air.

Maria hit the ground with her feet outspread, tried to fall forward, but the cut of the rope around her waist held her and she toppled sideways. At the same instant there was a sound in her ears and she knew somehow that this sodden, smashing impact was the body of her horse at the bottom of the arroyo.

At her side a voice said, "Sorry. Hope the rope didn't cut you in half."

She looked up into a face whose honest solicitude went queerly with the essential toughness of it.

She murmured dazedly, "You roped me."

"You had a blind bucker," he said. "You ought to have quit him."

"I—I didn't know," she began to stammer.

Abruptly she was aware that the column of steers was pounding past behind her. The dust of their passage was a choking mist in the air. The sound of gunfire was louder.

Another man appeared, leading a horse, his bowed legs stomping toward her carelessly. "Broke his neck," he announced in a cracked dry voice, "but that don't matter. When they fall that far they're plenty splattered anyways."

The man at Maria's side said, "Come on. Get up behind me. We got to be leaving."

She stood up shakily. "My saddle," she said. "I've got to have it. You—you go on."

The man at her side looked at her. His glance said, "Women! My God, women!"

Then he turned swiftly and yelled, "Jim! Pablo! Take point! Call up Lars and Ricardo for flank. Signal Bill to spread out and hold that outfit up for three minutes."

He swung on the bowlegged man, who might have been sixty or eighty—she had no idea which might be nearest. "Magpie, slide down an'—" He broke off. "Never mind, I'll get it." He swung toward the arroyo, a wide-shouldered, powerfully built man, with the impression of faintly irritable toughness visible even out of his back.

He slid over the arroyo's rim.

THE MAN called Magpie looked after him resentfully. "Thinks I'm too old for it," he rasped. "God knows why I ever tied up with a fool!" His seamed, leathery face fronted the girl defiantly, but while resentment was in his voice and manner, something else lived in his face—a curious pride, a dry and understanding humor.

She looked at him wide-eyed, and because the jolt of that stampeding mustang still ran through her she spoke without thinking, "Why—why you're loco about him," she said accusingly.

The white mustached face before her looked severe. "It's a-gittin' so that little gals is too fresh for their pants. I've run with this hombre some time, an' reckon I know plenty about him that stranger females ain't acquainted with."

From the bottom of the ravine, a voice called. "Let down a rope, Magpie."

The oldster jumped. "Comin' down, Silver, son," he yelled. And let his lass rope drop over the edge.

Maria Odlum stood breathless.

"Silver?" she cried. "Silver Trent?"

The oldster, Magpie, was attaching a rope to a saddle horn, to pull up both man and saddle. "Why not?" he said bruskly, as he led the horse off, drawing up the rope's burden.

The girl stood in her tracks, frozen.

In a moment, the other man came up over the edge, bearing her saddle and bridle. He tossed them to Magpie.

The drag of the herd had gone past. On the ridge the guns barked, the clamor of them increasing now. And beyond them came the muted snarl of other guns.

Something hit a rock and made a queer, high-pitched scream between her and the big-shouldered man. He appeared not to notice it. "Get up behind me," he said briefly, "Magpie'll take your saddle."

She rode that way until they came to the entrance to the canyon where she lived. Then she saw, with a rasping indraught of breath that they had already turned in there.

Into her canyon! How had they known about that?

The late sun made long shadows from the western walls to touch the foot of the eastern barricade. There was only one entrance into this place, except for the goat trail that led out at the rear. Were they stupid, or did they know about that rear outlet?

She followed the drag of the herd through into the mile square expanse of this which was her own box canyon, her slender hands about the waist of the man who rode in front of her, her divided skirt feeling damp from the sweated flanks of his horse.

Before the outspread, log-built expanse of her house, her rider pulled up.

The herd was ahead of them, spreading out into the canyon. Behind, she could see a group of men fanning out at the entrance.

She got down from the horse and found herself looking into

steady gray eyes. And suddenly she knew that this could not be the man she had thought he was. The face was tough, the jaw made of granite, but the gray eyes were too steady, too kind, to belong to a cruel and ruthless outlaw.

Automatically, her eyes ran over the scene before her and suddenly came to a halt. Her whole body went rigid. A shaft of the late light shone on the flank of a steer, picking out the C Bar O brand like an etching.

Her eyes flashed over the herd, finding the same brand, among others, spotted throughout the spreading cattle.

She turned blazing eyes at the man who still sat the horse which had brought him and her to this place.

"Those are my cows," she gasped. "Dad's and mine! You—you thieving varmint! You—"

THE BIG-SHOULDERED man turned to her, faint surprise in his gaze. In a gesture which seemed automatic, he shoved back the brim of his Stetson so that it sat on the back of his head. The movement disclosed a single thick lock of silver hair, running from the broad high forehead back beneath the tilted brim.

Maria Odlum gasped. Somehow she had not been willing to believe the old man's unspoken acknowledgment that this might be Silver Trent. But now she knew.

"You!" she breathed. "You!"

The big-shouldered man looked at her curiously.

"You're Silver Trent!" she cried in passionate accusation. "You stole our cattle—murdered dad! Damn you! I've heard about you. Tried not to believe the things I heard, because I was senseless enough to be influenced by the opinions of a lot of ignorant peons!" She paused for breath, anger flaring from her. "You've managed to fool them, all right!" she went on, "but other, smarter men knew better. And now I know better. Now I have the proof."

The passionate anger that shook her scarcely took account of the fact that he was swinging down from the saddle. But her hand whipped to the pearl-handled .38 which hung in a holster at her waist.

"You—you—" she panted, the gun centered on his stomach. "I've a damn good mind to kill you where you stand."

His hand went up, more than shoulder high, slowly, while his eyes stayed on her with a queer expression in them, half admiration, half quiet amusement.

"I didn't steal your cattle, lady," he said quietly, "nor did I—"

His left little finger flicked a little, as though by a nervous contraction. Involuntarily, her eyes went to it. So in that split fraction of a second she never saw the beginning of the movement of his right hand. She knew it only when it hit the gun in her hand like a snake striking.

The next instant, she stood holding her wrenched fingers, disarmed.

"Be quiet, child," Silver Trent said. "These cattle came from somebody else. If some of them are yours, you can have them back."

A staccato furore of gunfire echoed from the narrow entrance walls of the canyon, and then was still. Silver Trent's indifferent gray gaze swung in that direction. "You wouldn't think even a fool would run men into an alley like that," he said, almost pity-ingly. "Hell, I could hold this canyon with two men."

Maria Odlum glared at him. "Maybe," she flung at him, "but before you get out, you'll have to eat every stolen beef in your cow-thief's herd. And before that, I'll maybe be able to kill you, if the Rurales can't!"

A flicker of admiration wakened in the eyes of the big man before her. "I wouldn't put it past you, at that," he said softly.

CHAPTER 2
INTO THE TRAP!

WHAT SILVER TRENT had said about holding the canyon with two men appeared not to have been much of an exaggeration. It may have been that four were left there, but not more than that. The others came up almost at once.

Maria Odlum stared at them curiously. She had thought that she was choking back the rage in her throat, but it really was something more than that, she realized. Something was here that anger could not deal with and that had, perhaps, no basis in anger.

In the first place, this ruthless outlaw, Silver Trent, had saved her life. Which, she told herself tautly, was nothing. But also— and somehow this affected her more—he had saved it with an expertness which would have impressed any girl raised in the cow-country. That rope had not jerked her off a racing horse. It had stopped her not even as severely as a rope stops a calf which is not "busted."

It wouldn't have been possible to get her out of the saddle more gently and accurately. She had done enough roping to know that. And then, there was the look on that old man's face when he cursed his boss. And there was the fact that they had delayed to rescue her, even get her saddle, when guns were barking behind them. And there were the gray eyes of this tough-faced man, suddenly warm and kind. And now there was this crew....

Maria had never seen any group of men quite like them. Some of them were Americans, others Mexicans. There was a curious similarity about them, as timber wolves resemble one another, and an immense difference, and another kind of likeness which ran deep and which she could not quite analyze. There was a kind of careless unconcern, despite the fact that guns were at the canyon entrance, and there was—well, she might have said kindness, if that hadn't been patently absurd!

She listened to him while he gave them brief quiet instructions. Then he turned to her and asked, "Where's your dad?"

Her hot bitterness returned instantly. "You ought to know," she flung at him. "You killed him."

He did not flinch; his eyes hardly changed. "There's a horse there," he said quietly. "Get onto him. We'll look at the cattle."

The ride showed her not only her own brand but half a dozen others. "This haul comes from a gent named Ettore—Paco Ettore," Trent told her finally. "They were held up in the hills until their brands could be blotted or vented. Me, I never saw anythin' quite like it—two thousand head of mixed brands. Looks like the gent rustled them up, an' kept rustlin' 'em, without takin' the time to rebrand. It's right curious. Know anythin' about it?"

Instead of answering, she shot him a direct glance and asked, "How do you happen in on it?"

"Friend of ours lost some cows," Trent replied curtly. "They're in there. But we didn't expect to find all the others."

The girl gave him a long strange look. "Maybe the peons were right after all. They talk of you like you were a kind of god. You just did all this for a friend?"

The big shouldered man at her side shook his head impatiently. "We're human enough to help a pardner," he said, "but we aim to get ours, too. Don't go sentimental about it. What I want to know is—what's goin' on aroun' here?"

MARIA ODLUM'S cheeks flushed. "Nothing much," she snapped, "except that everybody's being rustled out, or run out. This is some of the best cow country in Mexico. But all up at this end of the Rio de Sangre valley there's been trouble. Dad held out almost the last of all. And I've heard that folks beyond here, down around Huesos Quebrados, have had grief too."

"An' the man behind it?"

"Maybe your Paco Ettore—maybe not. I've heard his name. But it's all been plenty tough to trace. We heard it was you and your gang." Her eyes were hard as she said it.

The outlaw appeared to overlook the implied accusation. "Around Huesos," he muttered. "Maybe I'd better take a look there."

He said nothing more and she saw nothing more of him after they had gotten back to her ranch house until after dark.

She wouldn't have known him then, except that she had once seen him swing into a saddle and had noted the queer, powerful grace with which he had done so. The urgent, even power of his muscles seemed an oiled mechanism. Only now, there was no saddle, only the bare back of a tough Mexican pony.

This Mexican peon in the peaked sombrero made the same characteristic motion in mounting and the power of the shoulders against the dark evening sky was the same. And with something almost like fright, she saw the mounted figure turn and ride toward the goat trail at the rear of the canyon. To her knowledge, no one of these men had been here before. How could they know about the rear trail?

Abruptly, all her suspicion returned. They must have known it all along. It must have been they who drove her father's herd out, en masse, and killed her father and his two vaqueros when they rode out to interfere!

She stood a moment while the physical world about her seemed to turn upside down. And in that moment of whirling and distorted vision, it seemed to her that the figure of the peon on horseback rode head downward from a livid sky, like a witch-bat swooping on its prey.

Her breath caught sharply and her nerves turned to ice. If he could go out, so also could she. Her woman's wit must be match enough for these desperadoes. He was going to Huesos and so would she! To betray him. To lead avengers to the rear door of this canyon while the front was blocked. To pay in clear coin for the death of her father!

ALMOST BEFORE she had finished these thoughts, the

14

peon was riding down the back trail, circling warily toward the main road to Huesos. His serape dangled from shoulders which now appeared less broad and powerful, which looked somehow hunched and crippled, one higher than the other.

The wiry little Mexican horse was so small that the man's bare feet dangled almost to the ground, and as befitted a small horse which bore such a large peon, the animal's gait was languid, even though the trot was deceptively ground eating.

Where he hit the main road, the horse slowed under Silver's restraining hand. His hoof-beats became shadowy sounds in the starlit dark. The road there was clear, silent.

Silver Trent pulled up. His eyes searched the shadows for movement, and his nose flared the air like a questing wolf's. It was as though his very nerves put out long feelers, probing delicately for the hidden death that might lie there.

But there was nothing. Or so it seemed.

He knew his danger. The men on his trail were not fools and did not take him to be one. They would know that he would not go into a blind alley. They would guess or know that there was an exit somewhere. No doubt they already had scouts out in the back country beyond the canyon to try to find that exit. And they would be guarding this road somewhere, ready to jump any wayfarer who happened along.

He knew that he might fool strangers, especially at night, in the dim flare of kerosene lamps, where his makeup would be almost invisible. His face, like his hands and dusty feet, was stained brown. His eyelashes were carefully blackened, so as to deepen the shade of his gray eyes. But there was a lot about the square cut shape of his face, the width and mobility of his mouth, the typically Anglo-Saxon toughness of all his features, which would betray him to any but a casual glance. He could not afford to be held up by suspicious men.

He let his horse go at a walk, slowly, along this road.

But this road was too quiet. The cicadas were still. The little mournful sound of the night hawk was queerly absent. And no coyote moved or yelped. Only the big black night flying beetles, who have neither sense nor caution, hummed their erratic, bullet-like course through the air.

And one other thing. A diamondback sounded his dry menacing whir behind Silver Trent. Behind? Why should a snake sound his warning after his passing instead of before? And the imitation was good, but not good enough for Trent's ears.

He pulled his horse off the road, turned him, and then jumped straight for the open, darkened range at his right. To the right, where the snake had sounded, a gun ripped the night silence to echoing shreds.

The bullet squealed in the air behind Trent's head like a lost soul. But he had no chance to think of that, because a crouched form ripped upward before him, cursing, and another Colt blared almost in his face. That slug also missed and Trent's gunhand whipped downward like a striking snake, the crunch of the barrel on bone a vicious under-note, soft and deadly.

To Trent's left gunfire also flowered, eight pistols stabbing the night with flame. The snarl of lead around his ears put a short savage symphony across the darkness.

The blacker line of an arroyo loomed ahead of him. He slid

his horse to a halt, then shoved him downward over the edge, as more bullets whipped about him. For a long moment then, he held his breath. There was no way to tell how deep this wash was—whether the horse must slide or jump, or whether he would break a leg or his neck in that blind leap. And Trent's neck with him.

THERE WAS a sweat-spurting instant when that held in doubt, and then the tough little pony hit the bottom of the arroyo with a cat's resilience. Trent's breath jolted out of him in shocked relief.

He swung the pony to his right, following the soft sand bottom of the arroyo, while the guns kept going, their lead harmless now as it sung overhead, but their sound sure to silence the swift beat of his horse's hoofs.

He remembered surely that he had passed the mouth of an arroyo in his brief ride along the road, and his instinct for terrain made him guess that this arroyo would lead back that way.

It did. And abruptly he chuckled silently. The aqueduct underneath the road was a great iron cylinder big enough to let his pony through. He pulled up, slid from the horse's back and led him under. It was close. The pony hesitated, tried to snort, and Trent's hand on his nostrils shut him off as he led him on.

Trent grinned suddenly in the darkness. For this arroyo made a U turn, and continued angling a little away from the road, in the direction he wanted to go—toward Huesos!

Now he could hear the shouts of the men, searching the opposite side of the road for him. Then a voice ripped out on the road itself, within twenty yards of where Trent was.

"What the hell did you shoot at, anyway?"

Another voice, worried and defensive, answered, "It looked like a Mex, but when I give the signal he jumped clean off the road, makin' a git-away. I couldn't take no chances."

The first man cursed disgustedly. *"Looked* like a Mex, an' you don't even know it wasn't just some fool greaser that scented somethin' in the dark an' got skeered. You damn' fool! You've give the whole trap away! If there's any of them Trent hombres within five mile of here they're plenty warned by now."

The voices died out as Trent, still smiling a little, followed the arroyo quietly leading the pony.

The leader's voice lifted savagely. "Come in, you blind buzzards! You ain't goin' to find nothin' out there."

And then, evidently because his voice was already raised and his temper out of hand, he snarled in a voice which would have carried a hundred yards. "I oughter gut-shoot you. Now we'll have to depend on the other gang fu'ther down the road. We'll go into Huesos an' keep an eye out there—see if we can't make up for your dumb play."

Trent slid quietly onto the pony, following the arroyo as it angled away from the road. So there was another trap farther on—and this gang was to be in town! His eyes narrowed, the jut of his jaw at once thoughtful and grim.

There must be more to this than finding some gents who had rustled stolen cows. The cows were back there safe in the box canyon, to be taken when anybody could force the entrance. There must be something ahead, some reason why Paco Ettore wanted so much to stop Trent or any of his men from going any further.

The next two hours' ride was tough, even for Trent, who had ridden this harsh land of Northern Mexico for more years than he liked to remember. But presently the lights of Huesos were plain before him.

CHAPTER 3
OUT OF SATAN'S CANTINA

HIS NERVES tensed. This town was dangerous, because it was the headquarters of the Rurales who had put a price on his head. And now it was doubly dangerous, because Paco Ettore's men were even now ranging it in search of him.

He frowned a little, wondering about that. It showed a little too much planning for Ettore. Ettore was tough—a half Italian, half Spaniard, who had made a sinister enough reputation for himself as a ruthless land-hog and killer. But Trent didn't think he'd be smart enough to look this far ahead. It gave him the idea that some other, some more subtle mind, was miked up in this thing. Whose? El Diablo's?

He shook himself impatiently. Maybe he was beginning to see ghosts. Maybe he was getting a little hysterical over the idea of El Diablo.

Esteban Bautista, who was known throughout all northern Mexico as the Devil, had been Trent's most persistent, deadly and shrewd enemy. The war between these two had become a legend. And though Silver Trent, by luck, skill, or sheer intelligence and courage, had somehow managed to come off winner in most of their encounters, still he had been underdog in more than one, and he considered himself always underdog in this: He had never been able to kill this El Diablo nor permanently break his power.

That failure and that continual battle had kept Trent more than once from taking advantage of the offers of amnesty which had been offered him by both the American and the Mexican governments.

His instinct persisted. There was something here which was beyond the straight, murderous instinct of Paco Ettore.

Or had he underestimated this man?

Taut, queerly hesitant, he rode in toward the flung handful of adobes which was Huesos Quebrados.

In an arroyo at the edge of town, he quit his horse and lounged ahead on foot. He appeared like an abnormally tall Mexican, who looked somehow crippled and old under the enfolding drape of his serape.

EVEN AT the outskirts of the town he sensed a tension, some feeling out of the ordinary. Possibly it was because of the darkness of the outlying houses and the lack of the free-souled noise of Mexican children, or the fact that there was no guitar to be heard anywhere. And yet, as he neared the plaza, it was clear that plenty of people were abroad.

He came up quietly through the lighted square and paused there, lounging indifferently, in the shadow of the wall where the alley ended. The plaza was crowded, but there was a perceptible lack of gaiety in the people who came by. Something in their manner, even in their laughter, made them seem taut, even dangerous.

For a long instant he weighed that in connection with his own case. Ettore's men must already be in town. Could it be their presence which had put into the citizens this tension?

The question brought its own answer. Neither he nor Ettore's men could be that important. There must be something else here—something that he ought to know.

He lounged out from the shadow and turned into the nearest cantina, his peaked Mexican sombrero pulled down over his eyes, his gait a cripple-shouldered limp.

The big low-ceilinged room was crowded, but the crowd was silent, except for one squat, pock-marked man, bull-necked and bull-voiced who was drunk and talking loud. At Silver's entrance, he broke off for a moment turning a glowering face to see who had come in. His small, red-rimmed eyes stared a moment, then he turned back to the bartender.

"… so what have I got to lose? What has anybody got to lose—eh, hombre? God's curse on them, say I! Why do I fear death? Does a landless man fear death or God or man?"

The bartender was making hurried, soothing motions and talking in a low tone. The rest of the room was silent as Trent limped, hump-shouldered, up to the bar. His mind, working with its usual lightning precision, hardly needed to have this scene explained to him. This pockmarked man was another like the girl's father, another like the ranchers of the upper part of the valley, who had lost their land. Or else he was a spy of

Ettore's sent to detect who among the townsmen were Ettore's chief enemies.

"Tequila!" he commanded to the sweating Mexican behind the bar. "And give tequila to my comrade here." He motioned toward the pock-marked man.

The pock-marked Mexican looked at him in surprise.

"Drink, amigo," Trent said grimly. "We are in like case. Who lives by the land can only die without the land. Let us drink—to Death!"

THE POCK-MARKED man swore, his small eyes blazing. "I take that toast and give you another, *camarado!* Death to those also who steal the land, and death to those cowards who fear too greatly to deal death to the thief and despoiler!" His bull neck swelled and reddened as he spoke, so that Trent knew he was no spy of Ettore's but a man whom fury and despair had driven to recklessness.

"I drink to that," he said and raised his glass.

But around them there was silence. Trent could feel the taut fear in that air.

"Where do you come from—from the north also, amigo?" he asked.

The pock-marked man hit a clenched fist on the bar. "So it is in the north as well?" He swung on the silent men at his sides and at tables behind him. "You hear that, *cobardes!*" He bellowed. "It is in the north as well! Where will you go? What will you do? Go to the north pole to find something to eat, a bit of ground to call your own? Fools, have you not the backbone to fight here and now?"

From the rest of the room a murmur lifted.

At a table by the door a lean man hit his fist on the table top. *"Por Dios!"* he growled, "what he says is true! Where will we go?"

The batwinged doors of the cantina swung inward, admitting a man garbed as a vaquero, with guns at both hips, a knife sheath thrust across his belly and a bandolier of cartridges diagonally over his chest.

Behind him, four others, similarly armed, crowded in.

"Por Dios!" the first vaquero said. "Is it true, then? You think it is true, dog? You think that you should live on land on which you cannot make a living? On which you must borrow? Pig!"

His hand flipped with unbelievable speed to the holster at his right hip and flicked downward, striking the lean man at the table in the face, so that he cried out and fell forward, sideways, missing the table top and plunging to the floor.

At the bar, the pock-marked man pulled a knife from nowhere and flung it at the leader of the *vaqueros.* The blade grazed his throat, leaving a faint trickle of red beneath the ear, and then the gun which had knocked the lean man from the table leveled, fast and deadly, centering on the pock-marked man's belly.

Nobody had seen Silver Trent draw. Nobody, in that confusion, could possibly have been expected to see a draw which no man, north or south of the Border had yet been able to match.

The guns appeared in his hand, from under the drape of his serape and the left one spoke. The blast of it appeared to knock the sixgun from the vaquero's hand as a hurricane gust whips hay from a stack.

The four behind the leader had stabbed for their guns, were

coming up now, blasting. One fast bullet whipped between Silver and the pock-marked man. Silver thumbed a lightning hammer that drove lead into the gunman's heart.

The pock-marked Mexican seized a gun from a man nearby and fired at another of the four who had drawn bead on Silver. The bullet smashed full into the man's chest, so that the blast of his gun went upward into the ceiling.

Silver shot another, while the fourth dived for the shelter of a table.

The room was in sudden wild confusion of breathless, panicky cries and the lunge of bodies jumping for any corner that might give temporary safety.

But in the same instant, the batwinged doors swung in and gun-handed forms swarmed through. Behind the first entries was a tall man with sloping-muscled arrogant shoulders and a mustache which curled from his upper lip like two thin snakes striking separately. Ettore!

His flaring, onyx eyes stabbed at the hunched, big-shouldered pseudo-Mexican at the bar, and he yelled, "Trent! Seelver Trent! Get him!"

His guns came up, but his men were in his way.

Trent shot one of them clear.

FROM THE sidelines a hunchbacked Mexican with blazing eyes hurled a chair. The chair struck along the first line of the newcomers, driven by muscles which crippled adversity had steeled. It glanced across the temple of the nearest man, whipped downward to stun the two gunmen next, and then drove its top agonizingly into the neck of the next man down.

The staggering and falling of the struck men created a confusion which made Silver's shot at Ettore miss by an eighth of an inch.

But there were men still pouring through the door. Beside Silver, the pockmarked man groaned and staggered as lead found him.

Silver's gun whipped upward toward the lights. The crashing echo of their explosion was punctuated with the crash and tinkle of glass—and then there was darkness, complete and absolute, as though the low ceiling of this room had pressed opaquely down to the floor.

Ettore's voice lifted shrill and ferocious in that acrid hush. "The back door!" he yelled. "Cut off the back door! And you outside, too. Go around! Cut off the back door!"

Silver caught the pock-marked man's arm in a grip that bit and commanded silence. Then he moved softly toward the front door, leading the other. They were both barefooted, so that their progress was nearly silent. At the door, Silver bumped into a vaquero who snarled, swung towards him.

"Quiet, fool!" Silver whispered in his faultless Mexican. "Do you want to draw Seelver's bullets on us."

As he spoke, he shoved the pockmarked man outward. "Go toward the back door," he whispered. "Cut off Seelver's escape there!"

The man hesitated, not wanting to quit the fight, but the urgency of Silver's fingers on his arm sent him out. Then Silver slid across the doorway, his chest rubbing the backs of men who barred it, dumbly oblivious of the fact that even so they were outlined against the outer light.

The room was still in a turmoil and confusion of stumbling, frightened men and the grimly racing gunmen of Ettore making their way toward the back door. No man dared strike a light for fear that it would draw a bullet toward him.

But Ettore was still bellowing orders, dodging from place to place so that his voice would not mark him as a target.

Silver moved toward the table where the lean man had fallen. He reached down, felt a groaning body, and then a hand. The hand grasped his with surprising strength, yanked him forward. He jerked free, using the whole power of his muscles. Something whizzed past his ear from behind him, sliced through his shirt and a quarter inch of shoulder flesh.

His hand went up and back, grasped the knife-arm. His other hand reached for the knife-thrower's body. It encountered a queer hump. He shifted it, and then knowledge dawned on him. He drew the hunchback to him swiftly.

"Amigo!" he whispered. "I am the tall one you helped. Help me now also."

The quiver of the hunchback's body was like that of a blooded horse. *"Dios!"* he murmured. "I could not tell in this darkness...."

"Lift him," Silver whispered.

His own arm swung upward under the groaning form of the lean man. And he could feel the lift of the hump-backed man's arms also.

They stood up and moved the two steps toward the door. The confusion had died down now into dead silence. Ettore's men had taken up their station at the back door. The front door was blocked by the five who stood there, and every man waited for a movement, a break that would start the gunfire anew.

Silver moved toward the door, bumping into a crouching gunman. "Fool!" he whispered savagely. "Will you let him dive over your head to go out. Stand up like a man. Are you a dog to fear this gringo coyote? Cover us, also. I take a wounded comrade out."

The man he spoke to straightened hesitantly. "Who…?" he began to whisper. But before he could finish, they were out of the door.

Outside, in the dim starlight, the pockmarked man lunged toward them suddenly. *"Dios* be thanked," he murmured,

Inside the saloon sudden gunfire broke out. Somebody, no doubt had moved and set that enormous tension off. But at the side of the door a voice yelled, *"Jefe!* I think they got out. I—" Abruptly his voice died, gurgling, under a smash of Colt-thunder.

Silver and the others were near the awed circle of townspeople, whose curiosity had been too much for their fear. And now he whispered tensely, "Run!"

CHAPTER 4
REFUGEES OF BLOOD VALLEY

T HE LEAN man had come to. He also could run, with a hand under his elbow. They burst through the muttering crowd and ran. Down a dark alley, and into a side street, expecting every moment to hear the race of pursuit behind them.

But the pock-marked man pulled up. "The crowd could see us. They could recognize me. They will not tell them which way we went."

The pock-marked man stared at Silver. He seemed sober now. "Maybe you haven't seen," he said softly. "Maybe we'd better go and talk to the others. But I say that is where they will look for us. There is danger there."

Silver looked at him. "Let's go," he said briefly.

"I am named Pancho," the pockmarked man said.

"And I am Silver Trent."

The pock-marked Pancho blew his breath out explosively. "That I know," he growled. "But if you were the Devil himself, I'd follow you after tonight. Someone has lied."

"*El Diablo*, perhaps?" Silver whispered.

Pancho stopped short, stared. "*El Diablo?*" he breathed. "But no, señor, it is Ettore…. That is—" His breath caught sharply, then he continued with an effort which was evidently caused by this new thought: "But—but señor, we have only heard of that evil one. What mean you, señor?"

Silver's hand shoved Pancho along. "Say that I am having nightmare, *amigo mio*. Always it is Esteban Bautista—El

28

Diablo—that I fight. So perhaps I see him where he is not, like an old woman muttering of ghosts by the fire."

At Silver's other side, the hunchback's voice snarled like an aroused hornet, addressing Pancho, "And if it is El Diablo, fool—does that put water in your coward's veins?"

But the lean man was silent and crossed himself, and the pock-marked Pancho made no reply.

So they came in silence to the refuse dump.

The sight of it brought Silver up, rigid. The dump was at the edge of town, yet within it. Humble shacks edged it on all sides—crumbling adobes of the poor that seemed to lean away from it in weary disgust, from its filth and its odor. But it was the dump itself which engaged Silver's attention.

For it was crowded. Stabled in between the tin cans and the piles of stinking waste, lined up along the banks of the filth-cluttered arroyo which bisected it, were men and women, children and animals, in a stirring noisome patina of misery.

There were wagons and donkeys and horses wearily stomping as they slept afoot. There were forms stretched out silently like exhausted corpses. And other forms were sleeping, also, but noisily, with the wheeze and bellows of the born snorers. There was that, as an undertone, but more than that were the waking forms, shadowy, yet enormously alive, and frightened.

Trent stood watching a long moment. Then he said, low-voiced and grim, "All right. What's all this?"

HIS DEMANDING glance went to the pock-marked man, but it was the hunchback that answered. "You ask, señor? If you did not know why are you here?" The question had a queer vibrancy, more like the note of a violin than the tone of a human voice. "But maybe you only guessed. It would be like you, I think. To guess of this misery, and to come to help. There are fools here that believe you have something to do with this. But I was not such a fool as that, even before you came! These, Señor Silver, are the miserable who have been dispossessed of their land. It has struck them all alike, like a plague of locusts. And so you see them—eaten bare; landless and lost!"

Trent's hard mouth drew into a flat and level line. "And how did this occur, *amigo?*" he asked softly.

"By the work of the Devil!" the hunchback snarled. "What else? You spoke of him whom men call El Diablo—"

The lean man's breath went into his throat whistling. "Chiquito—Montecito!" he breathed. "You are a fool. Be silent, mad one!"

"Mad! *Bah!*" the hunchback spat. "Do you think that a mere *bravo* like Ettore…?" Suddenly he swung on Trent, his pale, long face blazing. "You have heard, Señor Hawk—Montecito, Little Hill! That is my name, for the cursed hump on my back! And so men take my words for naught. I am a fool! I, Montecito—the insignificant hillock! But I tell you—"

Trent's abrupt gesture cut him off. "You are no fool, little friend," he said gently. "There are those who have humps on their backs and those who have humps on their brains. Of these latter, you are not, *amigito,* nor am I! I will think it honor to listen to you. But now, let us talk to these people."

Pancho broke his silence, his voice nervous, urgent. "Señor, I have told you. This is not safe. They will look for us here. Besides, we have come in by a back path, but there will be guards about here."

But unheeding, Silver walked forward toward an oldster who sat by the embers of a dying fire. "Friend," he said. "This is not a very good camping place. Why are you here?" The old man looked up at him, hard-eyed and suspicious, but there was something in the steady gray gaze he met which made him forget his suspicion.

"Because we've been fun out," he answered hoarsely. "Run out of the land that has been ours in my time and my father's time. Do you ask me how? I don't know. Some had mortgages which were foreclosed. Others were rustled into bankruptcy. Still others were threatened until their bellies ran weak and they sold out, because they knew that some who had refused had been killed. And so we are here, all at once—as though the earth had shaken and jarred us loose—because we do not know whom to fight, or how to fight or where to fight, or with what to fight.

"Señor, have you ever been outside the law through no fault of your own? Señor, it is bitter. There are men in uniform, with the majesty of the government behind them, and guns at their hips—men who hustle you from your house, and kick in the adobe walls and shame you before your women and your children—cursing you and knocking you about here and there, as a free man must not be knocked...."

HE STOPPED, breathing deep, tearing at the shirt which seemed to bind his scrawny, white-haired chest. "This has come to me, amigo," he cried. "To be shamed so. True, there was the knife at my belt, hidden under my shirt—to draw when I wished, and to die when I wished. But also there was the woman's hand on my arm, bidding me be quiet. And I—God help me!—I was weak enough to be driven off, and not once to draw the knife and drive it into the belly of a hireling thief! *Dios* grant me—"

A voice broke in, icy and menacing. "Grant you now an easy death, old fool! A death easier than—"

The hunchback and the lean man and Pancho had drawn alongside Silver, absorbed, as he was, by the oldster's words. Now, as Silver whirled, the others did also, and what happened was swift and brutal.

The hunchback went down, squawling in despairing rage. Pancho, hit from behind, tumbled forward, bellowing like a pole-axed bull. The lean man gasped, coughed and sunk downward as a knife in his back found his heart.

All this happened in the split second while two men caught Silver's arms, stopping the instant whirl of his body, clinging to him with savage strength.

In the same instant, a hurtling body hit him from behind, slamming him forward on his face. The men who held his arms went down with him, still holding, while the man who had jumped him sprawled on his back.

In that instant, lying so, Silver saw the old man get to his feet, snarling, and then saw the powerful body and brutal face of the man who struck downward at him.

It was the man of the cold voice who had first interrupted, and his clubbed six-gun missed the oldster's head and smashed downward on his left shoulder. Silver heard the sickening crack of the collar bone.

The old man's knees crumpled. He sagged. Silver heaved upward desperately. The man on his back tumbled off, falling on the man who held his right arm.

The brutal-faced man struck again. This time his miss was not quite as wide. The butt of his sixgun caught the oldster's head on the side—not with a knockout blow but with a cutting edge, so that a deep gash appeared at once, spurting blood.

SILVER, FIGHTING to his feet, saw that and cried out in a hoarse voice, stunned for an instant with the knowledge that the blow had chipped out a long segment of the old man's skull—that the oldster, dazed, yet still snarling, was down on his knees.

Silver's muscles exploded in fury. He was on his feet, now, the two men still clinging to his arms. He whipped free, caught them and slammed them together. Their skulls met and exploded with the dull plop of crushed melons.

Snarling, the man who had hit and mangled the oldster, whipped his gun upward for the final blow. And Silver, crushing the skulls of those others, was too late to help. The clubbed sixgun swung upward, and started down. But somehow the old man's right hand came up with the flash of steel showing in the dim light of the fire. The knife slid into his assailant's lower belly as though the taut flesh were butter, and then ripped upward to the breastbone.

The brutal-faced man screamed, his clubbed gun dropping from his hand. He clutched at his stomach and then spread his hands wide in a despairing gesture, while his insides began to fall out!

"Madre!" he groaned weakly, *"Madre!"*

The oldster looked at Silver and grinned, his withered lips spreading over gums without teeth. "Amigo," he gasped, "the shame is not now so—great."

He fell abruptly with his face downward into the coals, and died.

Silver cried out, his hand reaching to jerk the searing flesh from the fire, and then something hit him behind the ear and the burning coals seemed suddenly in his brain.

They made a light in which all this scene was bathed during what seemed an endless moment of paralysis. He could see the growling onrush of the crowd, hesitant, half-cowering, yet drawing in under the lash of their deep, frustrated anger. And there was a girl's voice lashing them on—a girl that Silver had seen somewhere before.

Behind Silver a voice snarled, "Back, dogs, or we—" And then the blow fell again and the light snuffed out in utter darkness....

CHAPTER 5
AS THE FUSE BURNS DOWN

H E WAS in a room, sitting in a chair, and his head ached unbearably. He held it carefully and tried to move his hands and feet, which felt queerly dead. They were dead; they wouldn't move.

A voice said, "Señor? You are awake?"

Slowly, painfully, he turned his head. It was the pock-marked

Pancho who had spoken. He was sitting in a chair also, with his feet and hands bound.

Recollection flashed on Silver. "Where are we? What happened?" he demanded at once.

"I don't know," Pancho said. "I think this is a cabin somewhere out of town. Last night, when they hit me on the head, I was dazed. Then I saw him hit you and I tried to get to you, but I could not move. The crowd was coming on, but they gave back like whipped curs when someone threatened them. Scum! It is well that they have lost their land. But a girl ran forward, crying your name, and cursing those who would not come to help you—a señorita beautiful in her anger. But one slapped her, knocked her down. Señor, I have never had such a moment—I, who had been struck at the base of the brain, and could not move."

His ugly, pock-marked face twisted with remembered rage. "And then," he went on thickly, "they hit you again and you went down at last. Of what are you made, señor, that you need two such blows, when one would have killed an ordinary man? And then the man raised his gun to hit you again when one cried, 'Alive, fool! Are you trying to kill him? He is to be taken alive.'

"Then, señor, I saw a sight that will choke this thick throat of mine while I live and remember. It was the hunchback, scrambling off into the crowd, like a rabbit scurrying through weeds. Ah, that I should have lifted a glass or ever taken the hand of a coward like that! It was then that the paralysis wore off a little and I tried to get up. But one nearby saw me and hit me again, and I remember nothing more until I awoke here."

Silver turned a wondering gaze on him through the haze of pain. "Alive?" he said. "Why alive?" Something stirred through his mind—a premonition, a queer vague knowledge.

And then a voice spoke from the doorway behind him. "So, *amigito carrissimo*," the voice purred, "you have come to life at last—for a moment?"

Silver Trent had no need to turn his head. All this had been foreknowledge, something more than suspected but deeply known from the beginning.

"Hello, Bautista, you scum of hell," he said quietly. "I figured you were behind this."

A whip of suppressed anger ran through the answering voice. "Fool! You will try to talk like a brave man, even though you are lost! I would like—"

The quick, furious step passed him, halted in front of him.

And Silver laughed. "You look more like a crippled buzzard than ever," he said, amused.

It was savage cruelty, for the man in front of him was deformed, his short body twisted and limping. He was dressed in black and his thin vulturine face made him seem like a crippled crow as he stood there.

AT SILVER'S words the thin, cruel mouth twisted in rage and the black eyes glared hatred. But an instant later, El Diablo had control of himself. The cold cruelty of his laugh matched Silver's own.

"My body is crippled, my friend, from your bullets. But my mind is sound enough—and a little too brilliant for you."

"Maybe not," Silver said quietly. "Your mind was deformed

36

before, else you would never have gotten the bullets. But I haven't had any idea yet that Ettore was smart enough to steal a valley two hundred miles long and fifty wide. No, I've been figuring on meeting that crippled, devil's brain of yours, Bautista. So you haven't lost anything by showin' yourself here, though it was dangerous."

Esteban Bautista laughed. "Dangerous! It is nearly dawn, my friend. Before the light comes full you and your pock-marked fool—the devil only knows why those witless ones saved him!—you both will be dead. I wish I had time to torture you as I would like, but I think this time I will take no chances. Your girl has ridden off, and I think that maybe she has gone for your men. I hope so, for I have set a trap for them. Not one shall live, for as you die, they are going to die also. I, Esteban Bautista, will have them hunted down no matter what hole they try to hide in. And as for the little girl that you've got, I'll take care of her, for a while." He leered like an evil-ridden bird of prey at Silver. "Remember these things, while you are waiting to die."

He turned to the doorway. "Bring in the dynamite, Ettore," he said, smiling thinly.

Silver felt the muscles ridge out on his jaw, the cold sweat spring out on his forehead.

He knew now who the girl had been—the girl he had seen the night before in the encampment of the dispossessed. It was the girl of the box canyon, she had followed him into town.

To spy on him or to help him? It did not matter now. The matter was that she would lead herself and his men into a trap that would mean death and worse to all of them. For his men, death or torture. For her, brutal and cruel dishonor and then death.

But the voice of Ettore came from behind him then. *"Jefe,"* Ettore said, "Let me torture him just a little before the dynamite blows him to hell. He has said words about me that I do not like."

"No!" Bautista snarled, narrow-eyed. "I've been cheated of my revenge before. This time it must be sure. If we delay, something might happen."

But Ettore said, his voice yearning like a lover's, *"Jefe,* let me drive just one pine splinter under his nails and light it. Just one, *Jefe."*

"One, then," Bautista breathed. "One only, and then the dynamite."

Ettore came forward fast. With his knife he slashed the binding of Silver's nearest arm, seized the hand and began feverishly to slap it. Silver, in a wave of agony, felt the circulation return to it. Ettore, hot-eyed lifted Silver's middle finger and shoved a splinter sharply under the nail.

IT WENT deep, half the nail's length, and he looked up expectantly at Silver's face. But Silver knew then that his face was a mask, without expression.

Ettore cursed, then whipped a match out of his pocket and lit the sliver.

Silver steeled himself inwardly. The agony of that first thrust under the nail had been bad, but the burning to follow must be unbearable. Yet he believed that there was no quiver in his face when the flame burned down and charred the splinter under his nail. Sweat, yes! He could feel it bead on his forehead and moisten the back of his neck, yet no muscle of his moved.

"*Carrao!*" El Diablo howled, in frustrated fury. "*Por Dios y El Infierno*, I'll torture him until he breaks." Then, breath whistling in his throat, he got partial command of himself. "No! I will not be tricked, cheated again!" He jumped forward squealing, and struck Ettore in the face. "Fool!" he snarled. "Are you tempting me to lose him—to be too late again? The dynamite, fool! And light the fuse!"

Ettore moved, fast.

Outside, through the window in front of Silver the gray light of dawn showed, the face of the day lessening the light of the single lantern, showing Pancho's face like a terrified, pock-marked moon.

A match flared behind Silver and there was the faint hiss of a powder fuse.

El Diablo's laugh seemed half drunken in its jubilant cruelty. "You'll have a few minutes to think it over, fool!" he snarled. "And remember, before you're blown to hell, your men will die also. And the girl!" And he was gone.

Pancho was staring bug-eyed at the sizzling fuse under Silver's chair. His face was dirty white and the sweat on it shone in the growing dawn, like the wet belly of a fish.

"Señor—señor!" the pockmarked man gasped. "There's enough dynamite there to blow the whole house to hell."

Silver looked at him. "Then we'll go with the house, and so we will not be without property in hell."

Pancho's breath drew in with a whistling gasp, and then

steadied. "Señor," he said, the rippling muscles of his face fighting one another, "I think I would not wish to die with a better man. It is an hour for me, señor—"

Silver had a stray impulse to laugh, but he could feel the sweat break out all over him, also.

"It is only death, Pancho," he said quietly. "That must come to all of us. How long is the fuse?"

"It was twelve inches, I think, señor—and three are gone," Pancho gasped.

Outside was silence, and the pale light grew.

Silver said, "Listen, Pancho, I will try to tip my chair over. Then you can throw yourself forward on your face. Maybe you can bite out the—"

"It is no use, señor," Pancho said wearily. "I was awake when they nailed the chairs to the floor."

Silver's nerves drew taut. Then this was the end. He threw his weight sideways and felt a slight give of the nails that held one side of his chair. "Try then!" he snarled. "Quick!"

But Pancho sat silent. "Señor Hawk," he said hoarsely, "the fuse is half through. It is no use."

SILVER YANKED vainly at his chair and the give was still small. Under him he could hear the low hiss of the fuse. And by the staring glisten in Pancho's sweating face he could almost gage its progress.

Abruptly, the Mexican drew his head back, relaxed. "What God wills, señor—" he breathed. "And yet—if I could get my hands on that hunchback—this *montecito* who is lower than a cockroach! If I could but—"

Something clicked in the door behind Silver, a scraping of metal against metal. His whole body tensed. He saw Pancho's startled eyes go to the door and then fill with almost unbearable terror as they shifted the dynamite under Silver's chair.

Still the metal scraped against the lock.

"Get out, fool," Silver shouted. "There's dynamite here!"

And then the door opened. Underneath Silver the fuse sputtered and seemed suddenly to race on, as the draught whipped up its pace. His jaws bit together.

There was a sudden plunging fall behind him, a curse, and silence. The opened, shocked mouth of Pancho gave him the first hint of the truth. Then a quiet voice under him said softly, "I was in time, Señor Seelver. The fuse is out. But it was so close that I think an eighth of an inch is too much even for a hunchback to seize."

"Come around, Montecito," Silver said quietly, "and let me thank you."

"There is no time, señor. Let me cut you loose."

"Montecito," Pancho said, "I have been wanting to get my hands on your neck—to caress it, Chiquito. From now on, there will be nothing too much for me to do for you."

The hunchback had finished slashing Silver's bonds. Now he went toward Pancho, "May I be protected from such caresses, amigo," he grinned. "Let it never be said that I was loved by a porker who has been too long in the ice-box. Sit still while I cut not your throat but your bonds. Did you think that I had run, pit-face? That I was as yellow as your smallpox? Maybe I shall not cut you loose after all."

A ragged blast of guns exploded outside. Beyond it, a faintly cursing voice sounded, and the farther pop of gunfire and then the pound of hoofs and yells.

Silver cursed and staggered to the window.

CHAPTER 6
WAR-CRY OF SILVER TRENT

H E COULD see El Diablo's men backing up, shooting, while a body of horsemen drove forward. His own men! He could see Jim Clane in the lead, yelling like an Indian as his guns beat a savage tattoo, and Lars behind him, his big horse somehow carrying his great blond head up to the fore. And old Magpie, cursing as much because he was behind these two as he was at the enemy. Pablo and Juan and Ricardo and Bill Lang and Doc Brimstone all roared above the sound of the guns and the girl behind them, riding like a slender graceful devil....

Then his gaze ripped away from them, puzzled. The Diablo crowd, outnumbering them two to one, were giving back. Why? His glance had gone to a ridge that paralleled the course of battle and he saw suddenly that it was full of men in uniform. He caught the glint of rifles. And now he knew what the trap was!

The federals, government troops, were there, waiting on the ridge, to let his own men charge through and then rip them to pieces from the flank.

He yelled, "Jim! Magpie! Turn back!"

But they could not hear him.

On the ridge, Silver saw a man get up, and he recognized the squat, greasy form of the local governor.

He had known all along that El Diablo must have bought the full cooperation of the authorities in order to have stolen the richest cattle valley in this part of Mexico. Yet it was a surprise to see this fat political crook so eager and subservient that he risked his skin in battle.

He saw the squat, pot-bellied figure get up suddenly, heard him scream, "Get ready!"

Silver started to yell that warning again, when a sudden sight cut off his voice. Behind the federal soldiers had appeared an up-springing ragged horde. They looked like peons, broken down vaqueros, and suddenly screaming women. There were old men hobbling and leaping about erratically, and young men racing viciously forward. And boys that were no more than children screeching like panthers let loose. In front of them bounded a queer, grotesque figure, his back humped, his spidery legs pumping like agile pistons. The dispossessed! The garbage dump crowd!

Silver shot an astounded glance behind him. He was conscious now that there had been a sound of running in that room after Pancho had been cut loose. But he had not known that the hunchback had gone out.

Even now, it seemed to him impossible that even that racing deformity who appeared now at the head of the variously armed mob, could have made it through some secret way in time to lead this charge. Yet miraculously, it was so....

And it was true also that the federal soldiers were lost. That raging mob falling on their backs stopped their fat leader just as he was about to give the command to fire. The troop turned, startled, panic-stricken, to be cut down, or to run for their lives, as maniacs armed with pistols, rifles, knives, pot-hooks, machetes, scythes, goat hooks and clubs, swarmed down on them.

They broke and screamed; they ran and died. Silver saw the fat-bellied governor turn and yell, and then Montecito hit him, slammed him to the ground. Silver saw a knife flash up and then down and knew what had happened. Knew that a cruel and corrupt traitor to his people had died.

But still his own men came on, charging. And the old yell raised, split this morning sky. "To Silver! Hell's Hawks for Trent!"

HE GROANED, unarmed and helpless. For even with the loss of the federal troops they were outnumbered two to one. And all at once he saw a new group burst out from the other flank—more Bautista men, boosting still more the odds against them, forming a living deadly wall between him and his desperately outnumbered saddle-mates.

Behind his first big group of fighters, El Diablo squawled, "Get them! That rabble has jumped the federals but that does not matter to us. We can still get Trent's hellions. Go forward, take them front and flank! Pronto!"

Silver saw all the danger, knew that the rabble above, full of rage and lack of discipline would kill the troops if they could, but would not be much use once they had vented their mob rage. He knew that before Montecito could organize them, Bautista and his men could wipe out his own bunch, slamming against the first force they had seen only a hundred yards off now. And another crowd of El Diablo's men were waiting to smash them in the flank as they charged by. Silver knew their lightning reactions, knew that they would turn to meet this flanking attack. But the sheer weight of numbers would be too great for them.

He groaned, helpless. And then whipped backwards from the window.

As he did so, he had one glimpse of El Diablo's thin, hating face, turned toward the adobe window, as though he could not understand why the dynamite had not yet gone off to blow Silver to hell.

And then Silver was back at the window, match in hand. The dynamite fuse was now so short that whoever lighted it took his own life in instant jeopardy.

Silver stuck the flame to the fuse and then raised the packet of sticks behind his shoulder. As the short fuse sizzled, Silver threw, heaving his load of death with a sure hand and driving shoulder muscles.

It landed in the midst of Bautista's troop and exploded.

Silver had a small instant to see them blown apart, before the hurricane of air knocked himself backwards.

He picked himself up painfully, to see a shambles in the valley street in front of him. Horses screamed and kicked. Men sprawled, some silent, others shrieking in agony.

He saw Esteban Bautista get up front the dirt and run, and he cursed because he had no sixgun in his hand with which to cut him down.

He saw his charging men swing left and rout the Bautista

flanking force. Then he sagged, the force of his emotions, the torture he had endured, and the killing blows on his head overcoming him.

And suddenly the room was full of sound and movement and the jubilant yet anxious voices of his men. There was a girl's hand on his arm and a girl's voice saying, "Silver, I am sorry that I doubted you. I did the best I could."

There was the sudden triumphant shriek of the hunchback, swaying and strutting before him, "Señor! Great Hawk of the Mountains, the crooked governor is dead. Ettore is dead. Everyone is dead except that snake, El Diablo, and he is fleeing, beaten. The people have back their land. The rustling, the stealing, the threats, and the crooked legal work are all over. The people have back their land! Thanks to you, *Jefe!*"

Silver looked at him. "Thanks to you, I think, *Montecito mio*," he said gently. *"Gracias, amigo."*

The hunchback stared at him out of great, widened eyes. "To me, *Halcon?*" he breathed. "You say to *me, Jefe?*" The great dark eyes filled suddenly with tears. "To me—a cripple—a monster? You say thanks to *me?*"

"I have told you that you have no deformity of the mind, amigo," Silver said gently. "And I think that but for you most of us would have died."

The cripple's breath went out from him a long sigh, and then all at once he seemed taller, not small and hunched but high and proud. He walked firmly and with a new confidence.

Silver turned to the girl. "And thanks to you," he said softly. "You—"

The girl's eyes were full on his. "I did what I could. But without you and your men and the power you have over people, even while you're being hit over the head, there would have been nothing. Thank God I got bucked off by a fool bronc, an'—"

Silver said, "No need for more talk. It's all over now." His eyes were veiled, but his hands were clenched at his side.

The girl looked at him straight. "I know what that means. It means that you're engaged—that you're engaged to danger, and maybe to some other girl. That marriage is far from your mind."

Silver's nails bit into his palms. "Yes," he said. "That's right."

"I haven't an ounce of gratitude in me." Maria Odlum breathed. "So when I say that I—I don't care about—anything, why...."

Montecito's voice whipped out like a thin whip to distract them. "He will take me, stumbling pock-marked imbecile!" he cried. "He will take me with his riders before you. For what have you done?"

Pancho's bullnecked rumble was menacing growl. "Careful, mosquito! I am more than you. It was I, and no other, who faced the dynamite with him."

Silver smiled at Maria. "It looks as though I had two good men."

"And one good woman?" Her voice was a murmur, hardly audible, but her eyes were eloquent.

Silver's throat was dry as he stammered, "I—I—why—well...." And then suddenly he turned on Pablo's lean disapproving face. "Well?" he yelled. "What are we standing around for? Haven't we got anythin' better to do than to stay here?"

47

THE SECRET OF
TORTURE RANCH

THEY WERE hanging an American in La Hoya, and it was typical of Silver Trent that he had put aside his own troubles to ride and see whether the hanging was deserved. For the name of the American had not been given. Only the excited rumor which had run swift and far south from the Rio Grande.

How far and fast it had run was shown by the amount of traffic on the roads into town—peons, goat-herders, small farmers, vaqueros from nearby haciendados—men and women and children, coming as though to a fiesta to see the gringo hang.

Behind Trent, Pablo lifted his lean, up-burning face to the hot sky and murmured, "Your sweet children, *Dios mio!* Is it any wonder I cannot keep my hands unreddened?"

Beside him, Magpie Myers said mildly, "A hangin's kind of like a bull-fight I reckon—barrin' the fact that the hangman often don't know how much danger he's in, whereas the matador can guess it purty close. But the sentiments of them that comes to look is much the same. They both want as much death as they kin git."

Pablo glared and was about to take up the argument invited by this implied criticism of bull-fighting, but before he could speak his eye was caught by a group of soldados at the roadside. He turned his glare on them challengingly and was hardly placated when they turned away from him politely.

"I shore hope this gringo ain't wuth savin'," Magpie remarked somberly. "It'd be a shame to ruin this town for us."

"It would be a miracle if an Americano *was* worth saving," Pablo remarked acidly. "But I also pray the saints that the miracle does not occur."

Ahead of him, Trent was hoping the same thing, a little grimly.

For the moment, this town was neutral ground. The authorities pretended that they did not recognize Trent or his men, nearly all of whom had a price on their heads. In return, Silver extended his protection to the town, both from his own men and from any other bandidos who might happen along.

But he knew, too, that the truce was shaky. Two things held the local commandante in line. First, it was not too healthy to try to collect the price on any members of Silver Trent's band. Secondly, the townspeople, like the people in the country round-about, swore by Silver. They had reason to have a good deal more love for him and his outfit than for their own government.

But there were strong forces at work to push the commandante and the town politicos in the other direction. It wouldn't take much to upset the balance.

Suddenly Silver's nerves hummed. Half a dozen riders had abruptly appeared on a trail which emerged from a deep arroyo and joined the trail road he and Magpie and Pablo were on. In the lead was a wolf-gaunt Mexican, with a deeply pockmarked face and a mouth that looked like a thin, cruelly twisted scar.

That was Esteban Bautista's aide-in-chief—Lobo Obrien. The name had been O'Brian two generations back, but all of

Behind Magpie's horse, at the end of a rope, the alcalde was a
squawking bundle as Silver unlimbered his guns....

the Irish that remained was a pair of queerly pale blue eyes and a fighting man's courage. The rest was as cold-blooded as a gila monster.

BEHIND HIM, Silver heard Pablo begin to curse softly in Spanish, mouthing blasphemies for which he might have knifed another man merely because they were an offense to the Blessed Saints.

All Silver's senses were instantly and vividly alert. Lobo Obrien was not the kind of man who would travel without a purpose, any more than Esteban Bautista, whom men called El Diablo, would permit him to do so.

So if Lobo was on the prowl about this hanging, the thing was more important than Trent had guessed. The chances were that it concerned himself more closely than he had first thought! Any interference would be a dozen times more dangerous.

He cursed himself again for not having brought more men. But he had had reason to expect an attack on his hideout by this same Bautista who was his greatest enemy. Inasmuch as he was short handed, he had not dared further weaken his force.

The two groups met exactly at the junction of the roads.

Lobo Obrien met Silver's eyes and pulled up slightly, his own eyes wary. *"Buenos dias, señor,"* he said sardonically.

Silver did not slacken pace. "Howdy, Obrien," he said curtly. Then he rode on, ahead.

It was a gesture which the situation demanded of him. He'd have lost face if he had insisted on Lobo Obrien and his crowd going on ahead. Yet Lobo Obrien could put a bullet through the back of his skull without half trying. The others no doubt could get Pablo and Magpie before they could turn. And there would be no trouble with the authorities.

Trent's spine crawled as he rode, though his hard, square-hewn face showed no sign of it.

At his left, Magpie pulled up alongside, riding with nonchalant ease of an oldster born to the saddle and pretty sure to die in it.

His white mustache did not even quiver now, and the blue eyes were as serene as the sky overhead, but there was beaded perspiration on Magpie's forehead, and Magpie didn't usually sweat. He was too old and dried out.

Behind them, Pablo's voice lifted, sneering: *"Jefe,* I will fall behind. I do not ride with vermin crawling on my back."

Silver and Magpie checked, turning instantly. This was fighting talk.

For Lobo Obrien was facing Pablo, his pale eyes venomous. The silence that followed was heavy, taut. Then the murder faded slowly out of Obrien's eyes. Silver could see the change of thought there, but could not read it.

"I'll remember what you said. Another time, hombre," he grated. And he turned his horse.

Silver turned, too, riding ahead as before with Magpie, but he was frowning. Lobo Obrien was a fighting man. It wasn't his habit to back down, even against odds. And here the odds in sheer numbers at least, had been in his favor.

After a second Silver shrugged. There must be some good reason for Lobo's backing down—a reason which it might be safer for Silver to know.… His mind returned to the man who was about to be hanged, he lifted his mount to a sharper pace.

A shot cracked out from the square ahead. It was followed by a breathless moment of silence, then a sudden confusion of furious yells and other shots.

Silver's spurred horse jumped into a gallop. Behind him, he could hear the pound of other hoofs as Lobo's gang got into motion. He swung his mount aside, checking, to let the Mexican go by. This was no time for the dignity of precedence. This was a time for maneuver.

LOBO'S PALE eyes stabbed at him sharply as he rode past, and their expression showed that he knew he had been out-maneuvered. But also there was some other, secret, knowledge there. What was it?

He let the Obrien men get twenty yards ahead before he and Magpie, with Pablo, rode on. Ahead, an alleyway opened, running parallel to the square. As the Mexican men surged past it, a figure staggered out.

Silver pulled his horse to a rearing halt and cursed, savagely. The man who had staggered out of the alley was Bill Lang, the ex-Ranger and, for the past ten months or so, one of his own men!

Lang's shirt was bloody and tattered. He was bareheaded, hardly able to stand. In his hand was a Mexican carbine, held by the barrel, half dragged, half used as a support for walking.

At sight of him, the crowd on the sidewalk had scattered. Now a voice squealed out in Spanish: "The American! He is here. Send the sol—"

The voice broke off as a townsman muttered an imprecation, and cuffed the speaker on the head.

But up ahead, Obrien's men had heard, were pulling up, looking back over their shoulders.

Silver jumped his horse to Lang's side. "Bill!" he called huskily. "What's happened to you, man? Was it you they were going to hang!"

Lang looked up at him dazedly, then recognition flooded his gaze. He tried to grin. "Reckon I was the—victim," he gasped.

Silver ripped out a curse. "Pablo," he snapped. "Take him up behind and line out for home. Magpie and I'll cover you."

He leaned down from the saddle and, with Pablo helping, got Bill Lang up.

The Obrien men had turned and were coming back. Soldiers were bursting out from a corner of the square a hundred yards away, and a squad of others began to erupt over a wall into the alleyway.

"Better come, *Jefe*," Pablo warned.

"Get goin'," Silver snarled, his eyes blazing with fury. "I'm stayin' long enough to teach that dog of an *alcalde* to hang one of my men, by God."

The first soldier who had hit the ground over the wall saw Lang on the back of Pablo's horse and yelled, snapping his carbine up to fire. A sixgun jumped into Silver's hand and blasted.

The soldier pivoted as though a heavy hand had smashed him back against the wall. A second soldier, who had hit the ground just behind him, looked wildly around for cover and then dived behind a barrel of trash. The others dropped hastily back over the wall.

Down the street hoofs pounded as the Varro men tore into action. Behind Silver, Pablo's gun slammed once and then he was away, with Lang hanging behind.

Magpie's old fashioned hawglegs slammed twice.

Silver swung in time to see an Obrien man throw up his

hands and dive from the saddle as though he were doing a trick riding stunt. At his side, a companion's horse went down. And the horse behind him came catapulting into him, throwing his rider over his head. Silver grinned as he saw that the rider was Lobo Obrien.

He tried to get a shot at him, but lead plucked at Silver's shoulder, reminding him that there were other guns to meet beside Obrien's. Behind the kicking, squealing mess of the fallen horses, a Mexican with the snarling mask of a coyote was aiming at him. Silver slammed lead at him, and saw him go down.

SILVER CAUGHT a glimpse of Obrien just as he dived for the space between two buildings. He missed a snap shot at the Mexican. But down the street, the soldiers began to advance cautiously, kneeling to fire as they came, and the flat snap of a rifle bullet sounded by Silver's ear.

"Down the alley!" he whipped out at Magpie, and jumped his horse for that cover with Magpie following.

The alley ran through to the street which entered the square at its other end. When they hit the street, Silver swung left into the square.

The *alcalde's* office was diagonally across, barely visible through the greenery which formed a garden of palms, flowering cactus, and shrubs in the heart of the square. On one edge of this green center a temporary wooden scaffold had been erected.

Silver drove his horse straight for the garden. The animal cleared low shrubbery, raced through the plants, hit the roadway on the other side, and slid thirty feet to a halt in front of the *alcalde's* adobe office.

At the big open window, Silver could see the man himself, a blubbery tub of fat, staring bug-eyed at him. Then, as the horse almost collided with the building, the man gave a squeak of terror and started to scuttle away.

Silver left the saddle before the horse had stopped. Momentum, and his leap, carried him clear through the window.

He whirled the *alcalde* around, caught him by the throat. "I'll teach you to try to hang any of my men!" he raged.

The plump Mexican waved his arms frantically. "Señor!" he choked, "it—it was not I—the—commandante—"

"And Esteban Bantista!" Silver supplied. "You slimy cockroach. Don't try to tell me you weren't in it, too."

"A-a-agh! No-ch! Military tr-ial…" was he choked.

"You lying scum," Silver raged, shaking him as a cat shakes a rat. "He's not a soldier, and he couldn't have a legal military trial if he was accused of killin' all the soldiers in the Mexican army. He was framed at Diablo's orders, and you helped in the frame!"

Outside, Magpie called, "Here comes the hull damn army, Silver. Better get movin'."

Silver picked the fat mayor up and threw him through the window. "Put a rope under his arms," he snapped. "We'll give him a little ride."

As he stepped through, and into the saddle himself, he could see the "army" coming, the commandante in the lead. They had just turned the greenery at the run and at sight of Silver and Magpie they burst forward, yelling and shooting their carbines from the hip.

Silver's guns jumped into his hands as he and Magpie galloped away. Lead hummed around them, too close for comfort.

The commandante was mounted and now, with a flourish of misguided heroism he charged forward, yelling for them to surrender. Behind Magpie's horse, at the end of a rope, the *alcalde* was a squawking bundle. Silver, still turned in his saddle, shot the commandante from his horse. Then they charged for the greenery through which they had come.

He slammed through a bush, yelling with terror, but his voice choked off as he hit the soft earth and got a mouthful of black loam.

Once in the half shelter of the open square garden, they kept to it, racing for the end of the square. At the end, he turned left, toward that section of town which had not yet had any excitement. A few slugs snarled about them as they crossed the roadway again and plunged into the side street at the end, but most of the soldiers had plunged into the garden, expecting them to cross the other way.

Once in the shelter of the side street, Silver pulled up and Magpie shook free the rope that held the *alcalde*. The fat politico had no more than half his clothes. His face was scratched and smeared with dirt. He was without breath and dazed, and somehow a flowering bit of shrub had gotten caught in his collar and stuck up coquettishly from behind one ear.

Magpie burst into an enchanted cackle of laughter, but Silver did not smile.

"If that man of mine dies," he told the *alcalde* grimly, "I'll come back and give you another ride—only this time the rope will be around your neck—not under your arms!"

CHAPTER 2
THE TRAP IS BAITED

ONCE FREE of the town, they circled and caught up with Pablo after traveling a few miles. Pablo had commandeered a cart and had put Bill Lang in it on a bed of hay. At sight of that, Magpie grunted. "We're goin' to have Rurale trouble anyhow. If there's any of 'em near enough, they'll run us down before we can get to the hideout."

Silver made not reply. The white anger was about his mouth again, and Magpie didn't press the point, knowing his boss. Trent was plenty cool, until somebody tried to pick on one of his men. But when that happened, this big-shouldered, easygoing outlaw went berserk. At this moment, Magpie knew, Silver would have been glad to face all the Rurales in Mexico.

When they rode up to the cart, Lang appeared to be asleep or unconscious. His face was drawn, blue-pale.

"How bad is he?" Silver asked Pablo low-voiced.

Pablo shrugged. "He is shot twice. Once from the front, high in the chest, and once behind, in the side. He could not stay on the horse."

"Lung hit?"

"I don't think so, *Jefe,* but close—perhaps too close. This is with the Blessed Saints." Pablo crossed himself.

Silver's jaw muscles ridged as he looked down at Bill Lang.

After a moment he said, "Pablo, you ride ahead. Get there as fast as you can and bring Doc Brimstone, and all the others back with you. We'll pull up before long and give Bill a rest."

Pablo pulled in a long breath. *"Jefe,"* he said sadly, "what have I done to make you angry with me? Always it is me who must run the errands, while others fight. Today I had nothing to do but kill a couple of soldados of that squad along the road, while you and Magpie did all the work behind me. Now the Rurales will come, and where will I be? Doing an errand. *Jefe,* I do not think these things are pleasing to the Saints!"

Silver suppressed a smile and clapped him on the shoulder. "Your horse has been walking longer than ours, Pablo. And besides, you will make a better ride than Magpie could. True, the Rurales, I happen to know, are far away. They will not get to us before you get back."

Pablo looked more cheerful. "True," he said, "Magpie is old. I had better go."

Magpie's face was crimson. "Why, you bat-eared, saddle-colored cross between a crucifix an' a knife-in-the-back, I can outride you the best day you ever had. Why, durn my hide—"

He broke off at Silver's quick gesture, but the harm had already been done. Bill Lang had awakened.

Pablo said with dignity, "I do not reply disrespectfully to the ancient. *Jefe,* I go."

He rode away, leaving Magpie speechless with indignation.

But Silver was looking at Bill Lang. "How you feelin', feller?"

Bill forced a faint heartiness into his voice. "Hell, I'm fine. I figger a couple of them hombres musta let their rifles off by accident. Because when them things called soldados takes aim at you, nobody's in danger but the bystanders."

Silver smiled, then sobered. "You better take it easy. If you could just tell me, short and fast, how come you're back."

"Jim—Jim's gone," Lang gasped. "Him an' his wife, both. House burned down. Nobody knows—what happened. When neighbors seen the fire an' come, there wasn't nobody there."

Silver's finger nails bit into his palms. Silently he cursed himself for not going in person when Jim had written to him.

"He—he was havin' trouble.... Don't nobody know details. Or they won't talk. Lars an' Ricardo stayed to try—to run down—some sign. I come for you."

His pale face took on a sudden faint flush of anger. "Some hombres tried to drygulch me outside of La Hoya." The anger made his voice stronger and clearer. "They missed, but then I got framed for a killin' in town, damn 'em! In a—hurry to do it, too." His eyes closed and his face went lax in exhaustion.

Silver swore in a soft undertone while his thoughts raced. A YEAR and a half before, Jim Clane, one of Silver's best men, had fallen in love with a Texas girl and had quit the gang to marry her. Through Bill Lang, who had once been a Ranger, Silver had been able to get Jim amnesty in Texas, and Jim had settled down on a ranch of his own.

Just six days before, Jim had sent Silver word that he was in a little trouble and asked Silver if he could lend him a hand. Silver had known at once that it must be pretty tough trouble, or Jim would never have asked for help. Jim was the kind that handled his own grief, and was plenty able to.

Silver had wanted to go himself, but it so happened that his great enemy, Esteban Bautsita, was up to something at the time, Silver had felt that his duty to his men lay in staying close to home. He had sent Lars Johanssen, Bill Lang and Ricardo, feeling that they ought to be able to handle Jim's trouble. But the fact that he himself had not gone had remained on his conscience.

And now that failure had resulted in disaster.

He rode beside the cart with his lips thinned and his eyes bleak. It looked as though Bautista was attacking from all sides at once. If he could keep Silver's men divided, busy meeting threats first on one flank and then another, he was sure eventually to find a chance to deal a smashing blow.

The enmity between Bautista, whom men called El Diablo, and Silver Trent dated from Bautisto's first murder of a friend of Trent's and his wife. El Diablo, so called because of his cunning, cruelty and ruthlessness, had amassed enormous wealth and a power which extended over a wide area. He was hated and feared universally by the people, but they were helpless against him and the officials his money had been able to corrupt. His only effective enemy was Silver Trent, who was as famous as an outlaw as Bautista was as a wolf that hunted around within the Brimstone Border.

On the surface, the contest had looked until now fairly even, with a shade of advantage on the side of Trent's Hawks. But actually, there was no evenness in it. Trent was fighting continually against terrific odds—odds created not only by Bautista's wealth and power, but by the fact that the Halcones—Trent's

Hawks—ironically enough, worked with a code of ethics, while El Diablo's ruthlessness stopped at no treachery or murder.

THAT THE outlaws had been able to hold up their end against such odds was attributable to two main elements. The first—and to Silver Trent by far the most important—was the quality of the men he had been able to attract to him. There wasn't a murderer or a *muy malo hombre* among them, but they constituted probably the toughest and ablest fighting men that could have been gathered at any time or any place.

They knew the hills among which they worked as some men know the faces of their wives. They could read signs that an Apache might have missed. They could hit targets that looked impossible to ordinary men. They were swift, cagy, reckless, and fiercely loyal to one another. Hardly ever numbering more than a score, they had been able to hold off, outwit and outfight, not only the Rurales—most of whom secretly sympathized with them—but the army of gunmen which El Diablo's money and powerful influence was able to obtain.

The second element lay in the personality of Silver Trent himself. To people who did not know him well, the man was an enigma. He was big physically, with powerful shoulders and narrow hips, but so were hundreds of other men. His square-hewn face looked tough, but a thousand others could match its toughness. He wasn't a particularly educated man, and as a leader he was by no means infallible. He was capable of losing his temper badly, as he had just done back there in La Hoya.

He appeared moody, because sometimes he would take chances that looked suicidal while at others he would back away from trouble in a manner that looked at least overcautious. Nobody had ever been able to accuse him of being yellow, but it certainly appeared true that sometimes he would go to a lot of bother to avoid an issue which another man who could match Silver's deadly gunhand would have forced.

But even to the short-sighted and the puzzled, it was clear that for more years than most outlaws live, Trent had managed to avoid the worst of the traps set for him, and to keep on doing business at the old stand. It was also plain that his men accorded him an absolute loyalty which few men in history, surely, had been able to command.

Those were two points which were thorns in the side of Esteban Bautista, called El Diablo.

The vision of that man's twisted form was before Silver's eyes as he rode now. Black-clad, El Diablo looked somehow more like a spider than a man—a spider with a narrow, thin-lipped, vulturine face and eyes that held the mocking, scheming shrewdness of Hell itself.

El Diablo had begun his attack by squeezing two smaller ranchers who were under Silver's protection. They had begun losing cattle. A couple of their hands had been killed in gunfights which virtually amounted to murder. There was no proof that the rustlers and killers were Bautista men, but Silver didn't need proof. El Diablo's technique was too familiar.

It meant trouble, and it probably meant a trap... And now this thing with Jim....

Ahead a peon's hut showed by the roadside. There was a shed under which Bill Lang could have shade without being moved from the cart. Silver turned in. As he did so, a faint movement showed on a ridge that paralleled the road. He had a glimpse of a sombrero, and then the hind quarters of a horse before both moved hastily behind some brush.

He stood with narrowed eyes, whistling softly. Were there more of them? Would he and Magpie have to fight it out here?

Somehow he thought not. Bautista couldn't have foreseen what would happen in La Hoya. More likely this was no more than a spy—one of Obrien's crowd—the one that had gotten away. Or Obrien himself.

He took a sudden decision. He'd pretend to fall into both of Bautista's traps. He'd pretend to take half the bunch to Texas and leave half here. But in fact, he would go to Texas with only Magpie, leaving the others to return to the hideout by a round-about route. Then, if trouble developed up the valley, Bautista would get an unpleasant surprise.

Silver drew a long, slow breath. He wished to God that Pablo and the others would hurry. He wanted to get started. If Jim and his wife had been killed, he told himself, somebody would pay a swift, high price for them.

But if he had known what had really happened to Jim Clane, he might have been less sure of that last point.

CHAPTER 3
DEATH TO THE
RIO ROBIN HOOD

THREE DAYS later two men rode into the town of Mica, Texas. One was big-shouldered and narrow hipped; the other an oldster, with a seamed leathery face and a white tobacco-stained mustache. As they rode down the dusty main street, citizens eyed them curiously and then with sharper attention. Opposite the town hall, a man with a marshal's star on his shirt narrowed his eyes, his expression at once puzzled and suspicious.

The puzzlement might have been explained by the suspicion, for there was nothing particularly out of the ordinary about the riders. They wore ordinary range clothes and the single holstered pistol each carried was not strapped down on the thigh, gunman fashion, but rode the hip high and conveniently as ordinary working cowboys usually wore them.

Yet there was something about them, a thing that, perhaps, the instinct alone could read—a sense of danger that lived underneath their casual manner. It was a hint of something wild, untamed and self-reliant—a thing intangible but also strangely strong and disturbing.

The marshal watched them stop in front of the hotel, then he turned abruptly into his office. He opened a drawer in his desk and began to go through a pile of old reward dodgers. After a few moments he swore softly and got up, hitching his holster carefully into place and loosening the gun.

"I wonder..." he murmured softly.

The big man's low-pulled Stetson would effectively hide an identifying silver lock of hair which had given a certain outlaw his name. The marshal had an idea he would like to see this big man with his hat off.

But on the way to the hotel, his step slowed unconsciously. The thought had came to him that maybe he wouldn't like to see the man without his hat, after all. Then, brushing the fear aside, he went stubbornly on... but the doubt kept coming back.

By the time he got to the hotel, the two strangers were coming out, accompanied by two others. The latter two had let it be known that they were friends of that fellow Clane, and they had been hanging around town for several days. The lawman's brows knit. He had had his suspicion of that pair, too.

The four stood for a moment talking and then the latter pair, the Mexican and the huge Scandinavian went down toward the livery barn, evidently after their horses.

The marshal was evolving a clever scheme to get the big-shouldered stranger to take off his hat without starting an immediate gunfight, when the man himself solved the problem. He glanced casually at the marshal and then removed the Stetson, wiping sweat from his forehead with his bandana, and then swabbing the sweat-band of the hat.

Relief flooded the lawman. The hair was all dark, there was no silver lock. Therefore, his walk, when he came up to them, had become almost a swagger.

"Howdy, gents?" he said. "Just ridin' through, or stayin' a while?"

THE BIG man turned on him easily. "Depends," he smiled. "We're friends of Jim Clane's. Got word his house was burned an' that he was missin'. Haven't found anything about it, have you?"

At the mention of Jim's name the marshal's face hardened. "Nothin'," he said curtly. "It's out of town anyway—not in my territory. The sheriff'll handle it."

The big man nodded. "We used to work with Jim," he said quietly. "We're kind of interested."

"Yeah? Used to work with him, huh? An' where was that?"

The newcomer turned steady gray eyes on him. "Looks like a nice little town you got here," he said in the same quiet tone.

The eyes had had no particular expression in them, yet the impact was something the lawman felt, like a physical chill.

For a moment, it held him speechless, then he found himself saying, "Why, yes…. It's a purty good town."

Down the street the other pair emerged from the livery barn.

The big man stepped toward his horse. "Maybe we'll be seein' you," he said courteously, and rode off with his wizened companion.

The lawman drew a deep breath, and all at once his face burned. By God, the jasper hadn't even bothered to answer him. And he—the town marshal—had stood there like a dumb-head and had let him get away with it!

He didn't admit to himself that something about those chill eyes had bluffed him out, but he was mad enough to kick a dog, just the same.

After a few minutes, a thought which had been trying to get through to him did get through. He remembered vaguely the description of a certain Magpie Myers, who was one of Silver Trent's men. And that recollection sent him on the run to his office.

Fifteen minutes later, he came out again, panting. Good thing he'd never thrown away a dodger! He had found what he was looking for, fifteen years back. Two thousand dollars reward for Ben Myers, called Magpie—old timer, mountain man, scout, sergeant of the Confederate army and cowpuncher. Wanted for bank robbery and murder in Tucson. Short, wiry, blue eyes, white hair and a white longhorn mustache. Known as one of the fastest gunmen and deadliest shots in the country. All law officers are cautioned to take no chances with this man.

Magpie Myers! Hadn't changed much in fifteen years, by golly.

And that meant that the big man with him was Silver Trent. What a haul!

But he needed a posse anyway, eight or ten men. For the other two must be in Trent's gang, too.

He knew at once that he couldn't get the men he needed in town. But this was Saturday, and the boys would be drifting in from the ranches before long. He began to stomp up and down impatiently, sweating. His eyes flared with the excitement of the bounty hunter.

AFTER HE had paced a few moments, he was aware of a rider who had pulled up in front of him. The marshal stiffened, staring sharply. Another stranger!

The man in front of him was wolf-lean, with narrow-set black eyes. He looked bad.

The marshal swore under his breath. If the whole Trent gang came in here…. "Who are you?" he asked sharply.

The rider returned his glance with a greasy attempt at seeming pleasant.

"I'm a feller that talks money," he said. "Maybe you could use some, if it was—well, if it wasn't against the law."

The marshal's attention sharpened and he quieted down. Money was something he could always use. "Say your say," he said briefly.

"Any strangers been driftin' into town?"

"An' if there has?"

"How many was it?" He paused, and seeing the marshal's expression, made a guess. "They ain't friends of mine."

The marshal squinted at him suspiciously. "You the law from somewhere?" He didn't want anybody dividing his bounty.

The stranger laughed harshly. "No. I'm just tryin' to give you a tip that might lead you to some reward money."

"That's different. If four strangers did come into town, an' I knew where they are, what's it to you?"

The stranger looked startled. "Four?" he exclaimed. "Only four?" Then after a moment he leaned over and began to talk rapidly.

When he had finished, the marshal's eyes were glowing, but after a moment they clouded. "Yeah, but if I drive 'em across the ford to you," he objected, "how do we cash in on the reward money?"

"We don't want it," the stranger assured him. "We couldn't cash in on it if we did." He looked significantly at the marshal and winked. "But they won't never get across the ford. We'll cut 'em down in the middle, an' you can wade out an' get 'em. There'll be ten thousand dollars or more, floatin' there like fish."

The marshal pressed his lips tight and made his decision. "You're on! I'll get six-seven of the boys an'—"

The stranger gave his harsh, contemptuous laugh. "You better get a couple of dozen," he advised. "Them ain't no cottontail rabbits you'll be chasin'."

He turned his horse to ride out of town. "We got twenty-four boys our-self," he said over his shoulder.

ON THE road to Jim's spread, Magpie said, queerly uneasy, "You kind of riled that there tin-badge, Silver. Wasn't no use in that."

He was thinking, suddenly of an old murder charge—maybe the queerest murder charge that ever had been made against a man who had no murder in his heart.

Silver shrugged. "I hate to let any badge-toter ride me into lyin'. To hell with him, anyhow. He ain't cut so very wide across the pants." Then he turned to Lars. "All right, let's have it."

Lars began to tell him what they had found out, from talk in town and around the countryside. Jim had bought his place from the estate of an old desert rat who had showed up one day loaded with gold and bought himself a ranch. Talk was that the old man had hit it rich and that the money he had spent on his spread wasn't even a good part of it. Likely nothing in it.

Still and all, Lars continued, the old feller used to disappear some time for a couple of weeks, and when he come back he had some money to put in the bank. Small amounts, but gold just the same. Maybe he had some little placer hid off somewhere and would go and pan out what he needed. Nobody ever managed to trail him.

When he died, there was a lot of looking around for a map to his mine but none was ever found, and folks began to guess that the mine was a joke—that the old codger, mebbe, had some kind of little investment that he would go and collect on from time to time.

But after Jim got the place, trouble began.

The neighbors were kind of hostile to begin with, because Jim was known to have been an outlaw, and Jim began to lose cattle. He figured it was the neighbors, and did some talking about it.

"You know Jim—he's hot-headed."

That hadn't helped any. When it looked as though he was about broke, he got an offer for the spread, not from any of the neighboring cattlemen but from a stranger. He turned it down, and from that time the trouble got worse. He lost more and more cattle, and one night his place was shot up. Him and his wife had had to fort up and shoot it out with the raidin' sons. By luck, the sheriff happened to be coming through with a posse on the trail of some buzzard, and the raiders had made dust, crossing the Rio into Mexico.

Jim had complained to the sheriff that he had the feeling he was being watched all the time, night and day. Twice he had caught glimpses of riders skylighted for an instant behind ridges, but they had disappeared like phantoms when he investigated. And in the mornings, he'd find fresh tracks where somebody had ridden around his house.

The sheriff had tried to check up on it but hadn't found anything out.

"He's one dese fat bunnies," Lars observed. "A politico. Don't bodder wid nobody, just who can get him elected again."

It was after that raid that Jim had sent for Silver.

For the rest, only tracks going to the ford down near Jim's place, and a burned house....

"I tank dese are hombres from American side," Lars said sagely. "Dey make tracks for *Mejico,* den cut back farder down. I don't like dese neighbors. Yah!"

Silver was silent, his eyes narrowed.

OH, YAH. There was one other thing, but didn't seem to mean much. A old partner of the codger whose spread Jim had bought had been found about ten miles up in the hills, dead. He was a prospector, too. Looked like he'd tangled with Apaches, because he had been tortured plenty before being killed.

Silver's mouth was grim, his eyes bleak.

"Dere's de spread," Lars said, waving a hand like a ham.

Silver brought up sharp, staring at the ranch house which showed below. "I thought you said that Jim's house was burned."

"Yah!" Lars agreed. "Jim, he built anodder, 'bout a month ago—up in that grove of cottonwoods."

Silver frowned. "Why in the hell would he do that now?" he wondered.

"He tell sheriff he want something he can fort up in, with the trouble he has been hayin', but me, I tank Mrs. Jim don't like dat old house for desert rat!" He threw back his head and

73

let out a bellow of laughter. "Wimmen!" he yelled delightedly. "Dat's dem!"

"But you said he was broke," Silver objected. "Jim wasn't the kind to make a money-fool of himself, or the kind to get stampeded by rustlin' or being watched."

"Yah!" Lars replied. "Wimmen!"

Silver rode first to the unburned house. Inside, the house was a wreck. Floor boards had been torn up, walls ripped out, the stones of the fireplace taken apart, even the roof showed signs of search.

Silver walked through it slowly, his eyes swift, photographic; the grimness of his expression growing. In front of the fireplace he stopped suddenly, his glance going upward. Up near the roof, in one of the beams which ran up on either side of the chimney, an opening showed—a small compartment, with the door swung open. Evidently, it had been cunningly contrived so that the door did not show when it was closed. Cobwebs, a further concealment, hung from it.

"By golly," Lars burst out. "I didn't see dat."

"I did," Ricardo said quietly. *Jefe,* I think that's where the map to this old feller's mine was, and I think Jim found it. I think the old man who was tortured told where it could be found, and that when they finally got in here, after Jim built his new house, they looked up there and it was gone. Maybe then they thought the old man had lied. That is why they searched everywhere else.

"It must be so, because otherwise they would not have had to take Jim and his señora away. And, *Jefe,* I do not think it was these neighbors. Texas men do not torture as Apaches do. I think the torturers came from Mexico, and that they are perhaps the men of—"

"Bautista!" the exclamation came between Silver's teeth softly.

Ricardo nodded. They stared at one another silently, the message of their thoughts going from one to the other.

"Bautista is right," Magpie grunted. "His sign is all over this thing from beginning to end!"

LARS' BLUE eyes flamed and color began to creep up into his face. "If he torture Jim," he raged, "I will go to him and put my two hands on him and pull him apart just like he bane a chicken." His great hands clenched.

"It will not be Jim," Silver said softly, "but the girl. That would be the way to make Jim talk." He spun on his heel, his manner all at once uncontrollably urgent. "We've got to hurry," he snapped.

"I think it is too late, *Jefe*. Once Jim has talked…." Ricardo broke, his voice shaken.

"We've got to see what we can try," Silver said impatiently. "Jim has a head. He may have thought of something."

He led the way fast to the burned house. Once there his manner became quiet, deliberate. He began to search through the ashes and charred remnants, over which reared the gaunt structure of the chimney. He was methodical, absorbed.

Once the others saw him stoop and look attentively at a slab of rock which showed through wind-loosened dirt. He scraped some of the dirt aside. It looked like the kind of rock which is put over an open disused well. But Silver did not linger over it. He went on searching, and as he searched disappointment grew in his manner.

"Yet he knew I was coming—or thought I was," he muttered aloud. "Maybe it was too fast…."

Magpie said sharply. "We got visitors, Silver."

He was looking toward the dozen riders who had appeared on the range half a mile away. "Hell! It's that damn law-dog. Posse with him. They're headin' this way.

Silver did not reply or look up. He was bending over, staring at a flat stone set in the fireplace hearth.

"Here comes trouble," Magpie said grimly, "if I know ways of ridin'. We better haul out or get ready to fight, one or the other."

Silver carefully rubbed soot away from the stone. There were scratches on it, faint, almost invisible. There was a circle with what looked like a bird in it, followed by a half circle with a break in the middle of it and just under it a wide V. After that was the crude figure of a man with what might have been horns sprouting from the ball of his head. Finally the letter J, hardly visible, faint and hasty.

Silver stood looking at it intense concentration in his face.

The thin crack of a Winchester sounded across the range and a spent bullet plopped into the ground in front of Magpie.

"*Vallejo del Arco Rompimiento!*" Silver breathed suddenly.

He whirled, his eyes blazing. "Ride! We've got to ride!"

"I'll agree," Magpie drawled. "Them gents is hostile an' willin' to show it pronto."

Silver shot a contemptuous glance at the posse, who were coming on at a gallop and appeared somehow none too anxious to get anywhere in a hurry. Then he led the way toward the river.

Shots whipped out behind them and the dull hum of a spent

slug sounded between Silver and Magpie. It sounded like a lazy bumble bee and Silver paid it about as much attention.

They turned left at the river, riding toward the ford. A growth of willow and brush screened the water from them. And the same brush screened from them a slight cautious movement across the river, where two dozen of Bautista's killers waited at the ford!

CHAPTER 4
EL DIABLO STRIKES

SILVER SLOWED, looking back at the posse, which followed at a distance. He and Magpie would have just time to cross the river before they'd come under fire. His eyes were suddenly wary.

Magpie growled suddenly, "What they hangin' back for? We ain't shot at 'em. I don't like this, Silver."

Silver pulled up. Ahead of them the break in the brush showed wide where the ford came in.

"I don't like it either," Silver said grimly. "There's a smell of El Diablo about this thing that gets stronger. Maybe we better cross some other place."

Magpie nodded. "Trouble is, there's plenty of quicksand around here."

Lars took a deep breath. "Silver, I like better to fight some skoonks than to fool with that quicksand."

The posse had halted, closer now. The two men in front raised their rifles and shot. Lead plucked at Silver's shirt.

Magpie swore. His Winchester came out of his saddleboot in one swift motion and was at his shoulder. His finger squeezed the trigger, and the marshal's horse dropped suddenly as though it had been pole-axed.

"Nice shot," Ricardo remarked grinning. *Jefe*, I know the river here. I think there is a place down behind the bend."

The posse was scrambling off its horses, taking cover in the bushes. Silver said go, and they hit the open space bunched and going fast.

A yell ripped out from across the river and a rifle barked. It was followed by a swift fusillade which broke out just as Silver's *Halcones* were disappearing behind the brush on the opposite side of the break. The firing followed them briefly, the slugs cutting blind through the brush and missing them.

Then the same voice lifted, cursing wildly in Spanish. "To your horses! Cut 'em off below, fools! By God, that damned wolf smelled us!"

Silver smiled thinly, recognizing Lobo Obrien's bellow. The river was not wide, and the delay in getting their horses cost Bautista's men their game.

"They'll be close on our tails, though," Magpie said.

Silver's jaw was set and his eyes suddenly tortured. "They'll have to ride then," he said, "because we're goin' to ride like we never did before!"

IT APPEARED that night, though, that Obrien's men were riding also. They showed silhouetted against the darkening eastern sky just after Silver and his men had changed horses at one of the secret remount stations that Silver maintained throughout the country. It had been fast trailing, even though the sign was plain in that flat country. But from here on, the ground began to rise and to break up.

Silver said, "Lars, you ride straight for the hideout. Ricardo you, too—only you take the trail by Piedras. Keep clear of towns. I don't want either of you to get what Bill Lang did. Magpie and I are riding to Broken Bow Valley. It's about four days' ride southeast of here. Pablo knows it. Tell him to bring every man we've got. We'll meet you there. You ought to make it half a day after we do. But don't stop to sleep."

"Broken Bow Valley," Lars said, his face twisted suddenly with the emotion he had been concealing for days. "Silver, you think Jim is there?"

"He's there, if he's alive," Silver said softly. "He left me a message. Bautista's got him."

Lars' great fists clenched. "Silver, let me come with you. Jim—he was my friend."

Silver's voice was suddenly gentle. "We can't take him alone—not just us four, Lars. You'll be doing him more good by making sure the others come, and come fast!"

The three nights and two days that followed were a nightmare to Silver. He drove himself and Magpie savagely, mercilessly. They stopped only to change dead-beat horses for fresh ones. They ate in the saddle, and slept there, when they slept at all.

By the dawn of the third day, the saddle-tough oldster swayed as he rode and his face was a gray mask of fatigue.

It lightened only a little when the valley opened out before them.

The valley had the shape of a bow—the bow broken by a jut of headland in the center. Just below this headland Bautista's encampment was plainly visible. A house and shed were there, the property of some vanished rancher, and the remains of a corral. About this the camp had been built.

By the number of horses and the figures he could see, Silver guessed that the encampment must number half a hundred men.

"We go around to the point," Silver said briefly. "From there we'll be close and we'll get a good look-see."

Magpie nodded. "There'll be a guard or two there," he commented wearily.

"We'll take care of them."

Magpie sighed. "Yeah, we'll take care of them."

The first one was far up the point, and he was easy. The second was at the edge of the cliff overlooking the camp, and Magpie, who could usually move like an Indian, cracked a stick beneath his foot as they came up to him.

THE GUARD whirled, throwing up his rifle as Silver jumped for him. And only luck saved that shot. Startled, the guard had forgotten, simply, to cock the Winchester. He gave one short, startled squawk, then the edge of Silver's palm connected with his temple.

He slumped, limp and silent.

From down below a cry rang out. It wasn't a cry of alarm, it was man's voice, high, thin and tortured. "Mama! Mama!" it cried.

Silver froze, the sweat springing out suddenly on an ashen face. Magpie's nails were biting into his palms. His eyes clung to Silver's, questioning, something pathetic in the horror which filled them—as though he were begging to be told that this thing was not what he thought it was.

"Jim! Jim Clane!" Silver breathed.

"Jim—Jim wouldn't holler—like that," Magpie said in a shaken voice.

"If he'd been tortured long enough—anybody might. God!"

The half animal, pleading cry lifted again.

Silver whirled. "Stay here. I've got to go down. I can stop that."

"Hell, boy, you can't do anything," Magpie said hoarsely. "There's fifty men—"

Silver said through his teeth, "You stay free, to guide the others—no matter what happens. Do you hear? No matter what happens!"

He ran forward toward the edge of the cliff. A chimney slanted down there, one he remembered from a former visit here with Jim—one which would cover him all the way down.

He worked his way down, holding by elbows and knees, ripping his clothes in his haste. The cry did not come again. Jim must have fainted.

He hit the bottom just opposite the cabin. There was a back window to the thing and the space behind was pretty well shielded by sparse brush. He crept forward.

Under the window, he could hear voices talking rapidly in Spanish, and a woman sobbing.

"Let me just have one more try at him, señor!"

Bautista's voice replied: "No. I think he is not pretending. It is not the way he would act under torture, screaming that way, if he was himself. I thought a touch of it might break through his bluff. But he screams like a child or an idiot. Any more may do him harm, delay his recovery. I've sent for Doc Alvarez. He's not as good as I hoped he would be, but he ought to know whether he has a chance to get well or not. Maybe he can operate successfully."

The voice was cold, meditative, as though Bautista were talking out a scientific problem for himself. And Silver's spine and belly crawled with the loathing that voice put into him.

"Then let me try the woman, señor." This other voice spoke Spanish as a Yaqui speaks it, and the slow, fumbling voice was hot with cruelty.

Varro's "No" sounded reluctant. "She can wait. I want her safe and unharmed in case he comes to. He'll talk his head off at the first hint of torture for her. Besides, I don't believe she knows anything. She'd have broken at his first yell if she had."

"You devil!" It was the woman, broken by grief and anger.

SILVER'S RACING mind took in the implications. At first, his sensation was that of relief. Jim was at least alive, and so was his wife. And neither was to be tortured any further. He began to wonder if he could get up the cliff without being seen.

That wonder was interrupted by a gasp behind him. He whirled just as the gun went off, and he felt the sear of hot lead across his shoulder.

His own gun jumped into his hand, blasted once. The wandering Bautista man grabbed his stomach and folded with a hoarse grunt.

Silver jumped away from the window. He was trapped. There

was no chance now to get back up that chimney. He'd be picked off before he could shove his way up two yards. And there'd be no chance to fight his way through half a hundred gunmen in front.

Running footsteps sounded beyond a corner of the cabin. They slowed, and then the man came into view. Silver shot him, and then called out, "All right, Bautista. I'm caught here. Call off your coyotes."

He could hear Bautista's indrawn breath, and then his smoothly mocking voice: "So your gallantry has gotten you into trouble, my friend. I'm delighted to welcome you. Just throw down your guns and come around to the front of the cabin with your hands up."

"All right. But call them off first."

An instant later he could hear Bautista call from the front. "Let him come safely, if he comes with his hands up. José, you and some others tie him before you bring him in."

A few moments later, Bautista stood in the doorway, grinning evilly at the bound Silver. "Pardon my precautions, señor, but you are sometimes rather overactive." He laughed and bowed. "Enter, señor. My poor house is yours."

Silver stopped short in that doorway, his stomach turning over at the smell of seared flesh that filled the air. Jim Clane sat on a bunk against the wall. His hands and bare feet were bound. There was a bandage about his head. His blank eyes looked at Silver without recognition, and his face was empty, slack-jawed.

"Your friend had a little accident—a blow on the head," Bautista's voice purred. "Very unfortunate. It seems to have

83

taken away his mind. But then, I suppose he did not have very much to start with."

Blind sudden rage surged up in Silver, shaking him. He fought it down. "And you tortured him—when he was like that!" he said thickly. "By God, Bautista I think some day I will contrive a very spectacular death for you."

"You sound sure of yourself." El Diablo's voice held sudden venom. "José! Take a scouting party out, in case some of Señor Trent's noble imbeciles are around somewhere. Find them!"

Abruptly then he swung on Trent. "You haven't got enough of them to take this place, but you had better hope that they make a good try at it. For only in that way will you die quickly, and not the way I have planned for you!"

HE LOOKED like a misshapen angry crow in his black clothes, for this man's body was twisted—twisted by Silver Trent's own lead as payment for that first murder of his. Enough bullets had smashed into him to kill him, but it appeared that Hell did not yet want him. So he had recovered, with a passionate hatred which had led him to spend the rest of his life acquiring the power to smash the man who had crippled him.

Silver had gotten hold of himself. "You've made those threats before," he mocked, "and they're kind of a safeguard for me. You're so anxious to see me die slow that you don't ever get around to killin' me at all."

Bautista snarled, spitting at him like a snake. "Menoxo, tie him to a chair," he ordered the Yaqui. "And see that you do a good job!"

The Yaqui went to work with his eyes gleaming. When he

had finished, he went eagerly to the brazier fire which was burning under the cabin chimney. The brazier was, Silver saw, filled with various iron rods. There was also a collection of thorns to one side....

Silver had not looked at Jim's wife, except for one brief, encouraging glance when he had entered. Now his eyes went to her again. But she was staring at the Indian, her face drawn and bloodless, the fascination of utter terror in her eyes.

Silver wondered curiously how, with that contorted expression on her face she could still seem lovely, still give off the impression of fineness, of tempered character, he had read in her at Jim's marriage. He wished he could say something comforting to her.

The Yaqui took a white hot rod from the fire and walked over to Silver, then looked expectantly at his master. For a moment, El Diablo's whole body shook visibly with the force of his yearning, but he shook his head.

"Soon!" he breathed. "But first I think we will have Mrs. Clane."

Silver cursed. "My God, Bautista, you're not going to begin on her!" he said desperately. "She doesn't know anything. I heard you say so under the window."

Bautista's thin vulturine face twisted into a mask of triumph. "But I think *you* do, my friend," he said. "The fool Clane sent you a message. It got through to you, but the bungling of those imbeciles in La Hoya. I think you know where the mine is. And, I—think—you—will—tell! Go ahead, Menoxo!"

The Yaqui moved swiftly toward Leila Clane. Silver saw

the fear in the girl's eyes, but there was something like relief, too. And it came to him that the stark terror she had shown a moment ago was because she was afraid they would torture Jim again.

Silver said: "Wait. I'll talk."

Bautista's eyes swung to him gleaming greed and triumph. "Ah! Wait, Menoxo. We will hear what the great Señor Trent has to say."

Silver flung him a glance of contempt. "You want that money bad, don't you Bautista? It costs a hell of a lot to support an army like you got to support. An' to pay taxes on hundreds of thousands of acres, and bribe officials in a dozen sections. The cattle market ain't been so good, eh? And I've hurt you plenty, myself. You're close to broke, ain't you, Bautista? By God, I'll smash you yet!"

CHAPTER 5
PRISONERS OF
TORTURE RANCH

THE TWISTED black figure stood poised like a spider about to strike, its eyes blazing pools of pure venom. For a second, Silver thought that Bautista would kill him there and then.

But the man's steel control won again. He waved to the Yaqui, "Get another iron. Señor Trent does not appear to have anything interesting to say."

"Oh, yes, I have," Trent's cool voice interrupted quietly. "He hasn't got any mine. But what there is, did happen to come out of a mine. A mine that has plenty of it for the taking. And you've had it under your nose for months!"

"Where?" Bautista snarled. "Where, damn you?"

"If I tell you, you swear not to harm Mrs. Clane?"

Bautista cackled, "You'd better take a chance on that."

"Very well," Silver said evenly. "You fool—it was buried under the house that your men burned down. And it's still there!"

Bautista kicked Silver in the mouth. "You lie, you stupid carrion. Do you think you can take me in with a story like that. The woman would have known about it, if that were true."

Silver said thickly through bloody lips, "She didn't know about it, because Jim was smart enough not to leave her open to that danger. Your clumsy gunmen had let him know that bad news was afoot, even before he knew what it was about. Then— my guess is—you had tortured that old prospector and found out where the map was. His friend had wanted to leave it to him as a legacy. Why, then I guess one of your men tried to steal the map one night from the top of the beam. And Jim caught him at it."

Bautista's eyes and Leila Clane's unconscious gasp told him that he had guessed right.

"The man got away," he went on, "but it put Jim on to the hiding place. He had heard about the mine and he only needed that hint. He found the paper and saw—that there *wasn't* any mine—only buried gold. And the gold was buried near the cottonwoods on the place itself. The old man didn't trust banks or anybody else, and his trips, when he came back with money were just a blind. He made a ride to some far-off town and swapped some gold for greenbacks."

A vein made a purple, pulsating knot on Bautista's forehead. "I still believe you're lying," he snarled. "Clane couldn't have dug under his house without his wife's knowing about it."

Silver laughed contemptuously. "He didn't dig, you fool. That's why he sent for me—because it wasn't safe to take the money out.

"It was buried in an old well, covered by a slab of rock, likely with grass growing over it and brush around it. When Jim found that out, he just built himself a new house on top of it, and waited. You're not too smart, Bautista. You'd rustled him broke. Would a man having a hard time of it build a new house when he had a perfectly good one already? Didn't that ever occur to you, even?"

Sudden chagrin showed through the raging hatred and greed in Bautista's face. He was silent, and Silver knew that he had won.

"Go ahead," he said calmly. "Go on down and see. The gold's still there. Your bright killer Obrien wasn't able to spring the trap that was going to catch me, but he can tell you that none of us had a chance to take anything away with us but our skins."

Bautista's eyes narrowed suddenly again. "Why'd he rave about this place then, after he had been hit on the head. Answer that one!"

SILVER SAID easily, "Him an' I had been up here on a fine quiet hunting trip. I know he always meant to take his wife here for a honeymoon, when he could get away. Maybe a bad head hurt will sometimes do that to a man."

The thought seemed to give Bautista a cruel amusement. "Honeymoon, eh?" His half insane cackle of laughter sounded. "Hope he's enjoyed it!"

Then he snapped into sudden action. "José! Tell the men to saddle up. We're riding to Texas. Three extra horses, for our guests. Hurry. And call in that scouting party."

He turned back to Silver, suddenly snarling. "If you've lied to me, I'll torture all three of you until you're nearly dead, and then boil you in oil."

The threat seemed to give him an idea. "Come to think of it," he said softly, "I'll have a little time for you now—while the men are getting ready. Menoxo, go to work on him. The feet first, I think."

Silver heard the girl draw a long shuddering breath, but he was barely paying attention. His mind was busy with the details of the plan which had flashed into his mind there on top of the cliff. It had taken him and Magpie more than three hours to work, Indian-fashion, around the valley, to locate the guards and take care of them. Pablo and the rest must be getting close in by now.

The Yaqui went swiftly over to the fireplace, took hold of an iron, then changed his mind and picked up the brazier pan. He knelt in front of Silver, and began to untie the ropes which would free one foot.

Once this Bautista crowd got started with its three prisoners, Magpie would lose no time riding ahead to forewarn Pablo and to pick a spot for an ambush. What Silver had to consider was how to protect Jim and Leila from getting shot when the attack came.

He had already begun quietly to loosen the bonds on his wrists enough to know that he could ultimately get free, despite the good job the Yaqui had done. But he wasn't working on them any more. No use tipping his hand too early.

The Yaqui got the ropes undone and Silver promptly kicked him in the Adam's apple. It would have been a feeble kick from an ordinary man, because Silver's thigh was still tied down to the front of the chair seat. He had to kick merely from the knee. But it was enough to send the Yaqui on his back, clutching at his throat and gagging. One hand fell into the open brazier at his side, and he let out a strangled yell.

He got to his feet, whipping out a knife, his eyes murderous.

Bautista's sharp command stopped him. "I told you he was lively, Menoxo." He chuckled evilly, not displeased at seeing his own man hurt. "Now go ahead—and don't bungle!"

The Yaqui recovered himself, but his eyes promised Silver a thousand deaths before he died.

This time he sidled up and took hold of the leg as a blacksmith shoes a horse. Silver submitted to having his boot and sock pulled off. And then, still holding him so, the Yaqui selected an iron and went to work on the sole of Silver's foot.

A sharp, sickening smell of burning flesh drifted through the room. Leila Clane groaned softly.

THE YAQUI looked back from Silver's foot to Silver's face,

and expression of stark unbelief in his eyes. The foot had not jerked, had not even flinched when the iron touched it.

Silver was looking at El Diablo, laughing at him. "You're a damn fool, Bautista," he said easily. "You've never grown up. Do you think an adult man minds a little pain? Damn' if I don't think you're more feeble-minded than Jim is right now!"

El Diablo's face contorted with fury. He moved forward like a spider jumping and hit Silver across the mouth.

For a moment, Silver's jaw was tight and the cold blaze of his eyes held death. "You'll pay for that, cockroach," he snapped. "When I—" And Bautista hit him again in the mouth.

Silver's visible fury disappeared suddenly. He laughed. "When the boys find out I've had to let myself be slapped twice by a half-wit," he drawled, "I'm sure goin' to come into some mighty big hoo-rawing."

For an instant it seemed that the vein on Bautista's forehead would burst and his voice, when it came, was a strangled squawl. "Burn him again, Menoxo," he screeched. "He's bluffing, damn him. He'll break, just like all the rest of them do."

The Yaqui seized another rod, and that strangely horrible smell of burned living flesh filled the room. Fresh red flashes of agony ran up Silver's leg to his brain, and he could feel the cold sweat begin on his forehead.

He turned his eyes to the girl. He grinned at her. "Don't mind this hombre," he told her, keeping his voice amused. "He ain't hurtin' me enough to matter."

His glance, as he turned it away from her, flicked to Jim, sitting on the couch. After an instant he frowned, puzzled. Jim still had the same blank idiotic expression, as though he were unaware of what was going on. His face was bathed in sweat.

He lifted his eyes to Bautista and found the Mexican watching with eyes which had suddenly cooled to cunning.

"Never mind, Menoxo," Bautista said suddenly. "You can't break him in the time we have. Give the girl a dose instead." THE YAQUI looked like a dog kicked away from a bone. "Señor," he pleaded in his fumbling Spanish, "just let me burn out an eye first. They always break fast after the eye goes. They...."

Bautista shook his head impatiently. "The girl, I tell you! Try her first, with the thorns. That will get him more than burning him. And then, just before we go, I'll let you have an eye—one of *her* eyes! Such big beautiful blue eyes, too. You should be satisfied with that, Menoxo—for the present."

Silver felt as though he were going to be sick. His thoughts stampeded, trying to find a way to divert this devil.

The Yaqui went eagerly for the thorns. He seized one on Leila's hands, untied it rapidly and held it in front, showing it to El Diablo. He gloated over the slender fingers with their carefully tended nails.

Silver fought his bonds desperately, felt them give again but knew that it would take him half an hour to really work his hands free. The Yaqui took a thorn and brought it up to Leila's middle finger. Then Jim Clane's hands came free with a jerk.

He launched himself an instant, hurtling, for the Yaqui. His eyes were alive, blazing. And the full impact of his body carried him to the floor, in front of Silver.

Jim went with him perforce, since his ankles were still bound, and landed with his arms about the Yaqui's waist.

The Indian reached for his knife, whipped it out. Jim caught his wrist, hanging onto it like grim death while his own right hand shot out, gripped one of the rods in the brazier.

El Diablo had snatched a sixgun from under his black coat, his hands moving like the lick of a lizard's tongue. Now he danced forward, to bring the barrel down on Jim's head.

Silver put out his free foot, got it under the edge of the brazier and kicked. The copper pan sailed up, hardly shedding a coal, and it landed square in El Diablo's face.

Bautista let out a terrified screech and leaped backward, dropping his gun.

In the same instant, Jim drove the rod into the Yaqui's throat, the white-hot iron biting through the flesh as though it were butter.

El Diablo, burned, half-blinded, from the smoking coals in his clothes, turned and jumped through the door, howling for help.

Jim lunged toward Bautista's gun, fell short of it, then lunged again. Silver tipped his chair over, falling on the Yaqui, from the seared hole in whose throat the red arterial blood was pumping in sharp spurts.

Silver's chair fell across him and awkwardly he rolled it, groping for the Indian's knife. His fingers clutched it. With one powerful upward twist he slashed the ropes that bound his wrists, taking an inch of his own flesh with them. And suddenly the doorway filled with Bautista men.

JIM GOT his hand on the gun and rolled to shoot, but Silver saw that he was going to be too late. One man in the doorway had his gun leveled at Jim, the other was swiveling for the kill.

Desperately, he threw the knife, saw it go home in the first gunman's belly. It was not enough to stop the shot but it made him miss.

In the same instant a gun blasted behind Silver, and the second Bautista man went down. Jim shot at the same time, thinking, apparently that it was a Bautista man behind him. He whirled awkwardly still attached to the chair, in time to see Magpie shoot again, while Jim's gun blasted in unison. The doorway was suddenly empty.

"Damn you, Magpie!" Silver snapped. "I told you to stay up there. Now you've ruined everything!"

The oldster looked suddenly embarrassed. "Silver," he said awkwardly, "the smell of that burnin' powder come driftin' up that rock like it was a real chimbley, an' I could hear Bautista yell. Then I knowed it was you this time. I—I couldn't stay up there. I'm sorry."

"Quit fightin'," Jim said dryly, "so Magpie can cut us loose. I don't want to use that bloody knife."

Bullets had begun to angle through the door and to smack into the walls of the shack. Leila Clane stood weakly silent, staring at her husband.

"Jim," she said faintly, "You—your head. Wasn't—"

Jim put his arm about her. "I'm sorry, honey. It takes more'n a little tap to hurt this solid bone *cabezo* of mine. I wanted to tell you, but I was scared you might miss the act some time—

especially if they started workin' me over. An' that meant they'd torture you. I'd have had to tell, like Silver did. An' the minute they got the gold, it'd have been finish for both of us!"

A bullet splintered through the hut walls and plopped leadenly on the floor.

Magpie looked at it disgustedly. "This shore ain't no fort," he grumbled. "If they get onto how they can smash it, there ain't goin' to be no cover here at all."

Outside, Bautista's voice rose to a squawk, cursing his men, driving them to move in on the cabin and finish it quickly.

"He'll do it, too," Silver said grimly, "Now that he knows where the gold is."

He stepped to the door, opened it a crack and shouted, "How did you like the coals of fire, Bautista? Why don't you come on back in, so we can tell you some more fairy stories?"

Bautista's answer was a stream of epithets, followed by a new storm of fire. Evidently he did not believe he had been fooled, or else didn't care—so long as he could kill Silver.

The firing broke off suddenly, and in the silence the sound of galloping hoofs was audible.

For an instant Silver's heart jumped with relief, and then the yells of Bautista's men told him that these were El Diablo's. For Lobo Obrien had come up.

Magpie showed a thin, worn smile. "That only makes it about seventy, instead of fifty."

Silver said, "Listen, Jim. You've got to try to take Leila up that chimney. You can rope her to you and help her up. Magpie and I'll cover here."

Jim shot him an agonized glance. "Silver," he said, with apparent irrelevance, "I reckon you know I never had nothin' harder to do than sit there an' let that devil burn you. Only, Leila…."

Silver stopped him quickly. "Quit! You know damn well I'd have done the same."

Jim turned to his wife, and led her toward the window. **JUST THEN** the first shot rang out from the cliff above. Jim jerked her back to cover, but no bullet came in the window. Instead, a steady, hammering fire began from up there.

Silver's eyes began to blaze. He jumped to the front door, careless of the torture of his burned foot. Through the crack he could see the Bautista crowd scattering for cover, leaving their saddled horses to stray.

Four figures only remained in front of the cabin, and they lay still. The others, some of them wounded, were racing for the brush. One running figure went down as he watched.

Exultation grew in Silver. The Bautista crowd was already forming a line of battle, to return the fire of those on the cliff. In a minute they would think to send a flanking party to get up behind the attackers. But by then it would be too late… if he knew old Pablo!

Silver whirled, running back to the chair and jerking on his boot. "Get ready," he snapped at the others, "there aren't more than eight men back there. The rest of 'em will be charging any minute."

The pain of that boot left him breathless for a moment, then he was up, limping toward the door again. He could hear

Bautista snarling orders, and saddled horses were still milling uncertainly about the yard.

"We can catch three without any trouble," Silver said to Magpie, standing at his elbow.

And then it came: One long, high-pitched yell and then the thunder of hoofs from the left. "Hell's Hawks for Trent! *A nosotros, Los Halcones!*"

There was something terrifying, paralyzing in that howled, exultant cry. These men of Bautista knew it too well, had heard it too often. Throughout all that Mexican country, men had heard it—either to their sorrow or their salvation. The hills knew it, and echoed it back as though they were rallying to it.

Leila Clane now, heard it for the first time, and cried, "Oh! *Oh!*" She sounded as if she were awed and frightened, but her eyes were shining.

Nobody heard her. The men with her were racing toward the horses. At the left, Trent's men were in sight now, Pablo in the lead yelling blasphemies, circling to hit Bautista's battle-line on the flank and roll it up. No more than a dozen men, but stretched out at a thundering gallop, and every blasting gun deadly as a rattler's strike.

The Bautista man at the end of the line got up cursing wildly, as the charge hammered toward him. Lead cut him down. And then the line broke, scattering, shooting wild. Men raced in all directions to get out from under those thundering hoofs and the deadly path of the guns.

THOSE THAT ran toward the corral and their horses met three new riders who were, in themselves, almost the equivalent of the other twelve—Jim Clane, and Magpie Myers, and Silver Trent! And always there was the devastating fire of the rifles from above.

Panic rode them. A few found horses and rode for their lives. Others bunched up in the brush, with the savage courage of cornered rats, knowing that they had to fight it out or die.

As the Bautista men had scattered, the Trent's Hawks broke up too, riding down individuals in the brush. But Silver's shouted orders brought them back.

"Jefe!" Pablo protested. "We could cut them to pieces!"

Silver shook his head. "There are too many of them—we'd lose good men doing it. And we've got a job to do. Come on."

They put Leila Clane on a horse and were under cover and out of rifle range before Bautista could curse any order into his men.

At the head of the valley they looked back. Diablo's crowd were still trying to round up horses. Not more than half of them were mounted.

Silver sighed, his face suddenly somber. "Well, we missed him again," he said. "He takes cover well and fast, doesn't he?"

"But—but won't he follow us?" Leila Clane asked.

Silver smiled grimly. "They've tried that before and found it wasn't healthy. They'll follow, but not close enough to run into any ambush. Jim'll have that gold in the bank before they hit the Rio."

Pablo looked at Jim. "Gold?"

Jim Clane put a warm hand on his shoulder. "About two hundred pounds of it, old timer," he said, "and that fighting charge of yours gave it to me—along with somethin' else that I prize higher."

He turned to Leila, "Honey, I reckon we won't have to mind much if somebody does try to rustle us out—not now."

Leila Clane drew a deep breath. "It's wonderful. I—" A sudden thought struck her. "But, Jim, it's not all ours any more. Silver—these men—"

Jim put out a quick, restraining hand, gripping her arm. His face was suddenly scarlet. At his side, Pablo pretended not to have heard, looking intently at some spot on the horizon.

Jim said quickly, "Silver, she didn't—?"

Only Silver was unembarrassed. "Of course not, Jim. Forget it."

Leila Clane was silent for a long time as she rode. She knew something had gone wrong, but she couldn't guess what. Later she whispered to her husband, "What did I say wrong."

"It wasn't anything, honey."

"Jim, don't lie. What was it?"

He looked at her squarely. "You can't pay with money for…" he fumbled. "I—you see, kid, they're our *friends*."

She looked bewildered. "You mean they—they'd do all this for us—I mean even though they are friends—and not take part of what we found, what they fought for? Why that's absurd!"

"They know they could take it all—if they ever needed it. It's just that…."

But Leila Clane had gotten it at last. The sudden flush that made her face lovely showed that. "I know," she said softly, "it's kind of like—you and me…. Oh, Jim, I'm a fool!"

He grinned at her with his eyes warming. "Like hell you are!" he said.

And Silver, looking back and seeing their faces, knew that it was all right. Only, for a moment, there was a sudden, empty loneliness in him.

Then somebody in the back of the column struck up with a song which a later and lesser bandit was one day to make his own—*La Cucaracha.* One by one the voices joined in, hot and gay with the wine of battle and victory. Silver drew a deep breath and his deep, clear baritone hit in with chorus. His loneliness was gone....

ONE LAST RAID FOR
TRENT'S HELL-HAWKS!

E VEN THE land seemed different from Mexico, and the smell of it was different. Magpie Myers' nose sniffed it like that of an old hound dog, wistfully, with the memory of other days sharp within him.

A buggy passed in the darkness and the voices and laughter that came from it were American, not Mexican.

"Sparkin'," Magpie snorted. But he remembered other nights under stars like these, and another girl....

The thought came to him that it would be a fine thing if a man could settle down in his own country on a spread of his own, to live out his remaining days. Not troubled by the law, not running like a hunted fox. He wondered if that girl....

At that point, he shook himself querulously. "Day-dreamin' like a old fool!" he snorted. Their was no limitation on a charge of murder. Ben Myers, who was called Magpie for some forgotten reason, could not live long enough to erase that first indelible charge. No piling up of time could buy him peace nor amnesty from the law.

Ahead, a shaft of light from an adobe building lay across the road as though it came from top and bottom of batwing doors. Beyond, the lights of Tucson were still a good mile and a half away.

Magpie hesitated only briefly as he came opposite the weath-

Men began to boil from the
rear of the building....

ered sign, "Final Last Chance." He wanted a drink and he wanted information. He might get both more safely here than in town.

He got down from the saddle and cat-footed to the side of the building. A grimy, fly-specked window showed him a bartender and two customers. He didn't know any of them, and therefore it was likely that he wouldn't be recognized.

He went around to the door and pushed inside. The customers looked at him with indifference, and the bartender with professional friendliness.

"Howdy, gents," Magpie said genially. "I thought mebbe I'd take a leetle snake-juice for my health's sake. Seein' that I hate to drink alone, I'm plumb glad to find you here. You name it, an' the p'ison's yourn."

The customers' indifference underwent a change for the better. They were not the men, they said, to offend a gent by refusing to drink with him.

WHEN THE formalities had been completed, Magpie said, "I'm lookin' for a young feller named Long—Dave Long—that's a law-shark here in Tucson. Could any of you gents tell me where he lives when he's home. I've kind of missed out on his office hours."

The bartender said, "Dave Long—now let me see...."

But one of the customers cut in. "Sure, I know him. He lives right near me—him an' his mother. You go on up the road to town until you come to the second cross street—kind of a wide one with cotton-woods along it—and turn right. It's about the third house down. They're nice folks."

Magpie slid his watch out of his pocket and looked at it. "Reckon it's not too late. Don't know if he'll want to do business after office hours, but a man can allus try."

He wanted to emphasize the impression that he didn't know Dave Long.

The other man laughed. "Reckon Dave ain't got so much business he'll want to turn any down. What time is it, anyway?"

Magpie took out the watch again. "She's ten after nine, exact," he said.

The bartender pulled out his own watch and nodded, "Right on the dot," he said. It was evidently a new watch of which he was considerably proud.

"Nice looking watch you got there," the customer complimented Magpie.

"Yeah," Magpie lied easily. "Give to me for Christmas. Ain't been a half minute out of the way in fifteen years."

Actually he had taken it from a fat Mexican *haciendero* who had incurred Silver Trent's displeasure by oppressing the peons. Magpie remembered how the man's fat belly had quivered with terror as he was relieved of the watch, and suppressed a grin at the recollection.

But after he had paid for the drinks and ridden off he was still wondering if Dave Long's mother had ever remarried....

The thought nagged him, and it may have been the reason his normally acute senses were not as customarily alert to danger half a mile along the road.

HE HAD a brief glimpse of movement from the low bluff by which the road ran and automatically drove steel to his horse as his hands flicked toward his guns. But that was too late. The loop of a lasso rope settled about his elbows and he was jerked from the saddle, landing hard. His arms were caught tight to his sides, his guns still half in leather.

The fall jarred the breath out of him for a moment, and before he could recover, half a dozen swift black forms were on him. They took his guns and jerked him to his feet.

Not a word had been spoken. But now a voice said impatiently in Spanish. "All right, give it to him, you fool."

Half a second later something exploded behind Magpie's ear. The explosion set off blinding lights inside his head—lights which flared high, turned red and died away fast into dead blackness....

He came to life again slowly, aware vaguely of a light in his eyes and voices around him. His head ached violently and the light was unpleasant. He tried to turn away his head.

"He's coming to," a voice said. "Hey, wake up, you!" The command was followed by a hard slap on the face. The slap set off a hammering hell in Magpie's head and wrenched an involuntary groan from him. But it put anger into him, too, and he sat up abruptly, though still dazed.

The movement brought a new kind of pain, lancing from his thigh this time, and he became aware of a sticky wetness there.

The light, he saw, was a lantern and there were a couple of other lanterns nearby. One of the men had a marshal's badge on his shirt which glinted in the lamplight.

"He ain't hurt bad," someone remarked.

"Yeah. We got one of the murderin' skunks, anyhow."

Magpie wondered who they were talking about.

Another voice spoke up from the edge of the crowd. "I say we ought to string him up right here an' now."

There was a sudden, angry murmur of assent.

The marshal turned his head toward the speaker and said irritably. "We won't have any more of that talk. Unless my eyes have gone back on me, this is Magpie Myers. He'll hang for this, all right, without you troublin' yourself." He leaned down and jerked Magpie to his feet. "Come on, you."

Magpie nearly went down again when his weight came on his leg. When the pain of that had passed, steel bracelets were on his wrists.

The marshal said, "All right, make way there."

There was an undernote of uneasiness in the sharpness of his voice, as though he wasn't sure he'd be allowed to take his prisoner away.

The crowd gave way, reluctantly. Through the space it made, Magpie saw what was evidently a stage-coach. One of the lead horses was down and several men were busy getting the harness off him.

By the wheel of the stage a figure lay on his back, the curious air of being shrunken in his clothes giving unmistakable evidence that he was dead. Somebody had put a bandanna over his face. On the seat of the coach, another figure slumped, motionless.

ANOTHER GROUP of men surrounded a man who looked like a cigar or whisky drummer. His face showed pale and sweating in the glow of one of the carriage lights.

The drummer said, "No, sir. Not a doubt in the world about its bein' the Silver Trent gang. Like I was tellin' these gents, one of 'em made a slip an' called Trent's name.

"He said, 'Silver, what do you want to do with this damn passenger?' Just like that—cold as ice!" His voice shook as though the memory of that terror still made him quake. "A big fellow answered," went on excitedly. " 'Let the fool go,' he says. 'He's harml—' "

He broke off suddenly, embarrassed. "He's—er—unarmed," he finished lamely.

Somebody snickered. The sheriff jerked Magpie violently by the arm, moving him toward his horse.

Magpie got into the saddle with difficulty, helped by a deputy. The effort caused a gush of the warm stickiness from his thigh.

The deputy stepped back and swore, his hands and shirt front stained with blood. "He's bleedin' pretty bad, Bill," he said. "Maybe we ought to tie up that leg."

The marshal was already in the saddle. "I hope the son bleeds to death," he growled. "Save me havin' a lynchin' on my record. Come on, ride out of here."

The deputy got into the saddle fast. "Mebbe you're right," he said. "The way this town is worked up...."

Magpie frowned, puzzled. "Look," he said finally. "What's this about? I didn't have anything to do with it."

"Shut up," the marshal snarled at him. "By God, you try playin' innercent with me an' I'll bat your damn haid off."

Magpie shut up. His head was getting a little clearer—clear

enough to know that the story he had to tell would have no chance at all of being believed.

"I reckon it was Pete that shot him," the deputy said, after they had ridden awhile. There was one shot fired out of his gun and one out of Rawhide's. But I reckon Pete was the best shot. Pity he didn't plug him in his dirty heart instead of in the laig."

He'd known he'd been shot. But by one of the men on the coach? A sudden memory came to him—a voice saying, "Give it to him, you fool." The voice had been familiar.

But why frame him. Why frame Silver and the rest of the gang?

By the time they had gotten to the jail, he was faint with loss of blood.

They searched him, emptied his pockets, and put him in a cell. After a little while a doctor came in and bound up his leg. The bullet had missed the bone and gone all the way through. He felt Magpie's head and said that it was not fractured. "Slight concussion," he said. "You must have fallen good and hard."

Magpie asked him for a drink and got it—a good slug.

"Help you to sleep," the doctor said. "That's what you need now."

But when he was gone, Magpie yelled for the jailer. "Get me a lawyer," he demanded. "I want a man named Long—Dave Long. A young feller."

The jailer sneered. "You don't need no law shark. What you need is a blacksmith to make you an iron neck."

"Just the same," Magpie insisted stubbornly, "I got a right

to him. You send for him. You don't, an' it won't help your case none in court."

The deputy who had ridden in with Magpie came to the door of the office. "I reckon he's right on that last," he said. "I'll get Dave for him—though I don't think Dave or anybody else will handle the case."

Magpie sat down the single bunk, his head in his hands. It seemed true enough: No lawyer could help him out of this. But he had to see Dave—tell him that now he couldn't help.

CHAPTER 2
THE TRAP IS BAITED

AFTER A few minutes, he began to regret not having waited for morning. What he wanted most to do now was to sleep. From time to time during the next ten minutes he nodded, but something was nagging at his mind—something that jerked him back to consciousness at intervals.

And then Dave Long was there, standing outside the bars.

"Magpie!" Dave Long said. "Magpie!"

Magpie shook his head violently, and the jailer turned and gave Dave Long a hard, surprised glance, but the youngster paid no attention to either. "Old timer," he said, with unconcealed emotion, "I'm sorry to see you *here,* but I'm sure glad to see you!"

He stepped through the opened cell door and shook Magpie's hand hard.

The kid had his mother's eyes, Magpie saw, but the jaw was old Buff Long's. It gave him a queer feeling.

110

The jailer was standing by the cell door staring. Dave Long turned on him brusquely. "All right," he snapped. "Take those big ears of yours out to the office and shut the door."

The man started and obeyed.

Magpie said: "You shouldn't have seemed so friendly with me. I'm kind of smallpox around here."

"To hell with that," Dave Long said impatiently. "I'm not liable to cold-shoulder a friend like you, no matter what Tuscon thinks."

Magpie looked at him, pride growing in him. The kid stood straight and foursquare.

Dave Long saw the look in his eyes and said: "I know what you're thinking. You're rememberin' that the last time you saw me I was a kid of ten, crippled, paralyzed from the waist down. Oh, don't think I don't know it was you that sent us the money for the operation that let me walk again. And the money to put me through law school.

"As soon as I got old enough to talk turkey, I got it out of old Pete Sorenson. That tall tale about him inheritin' the money from an old uncle and lending it to us wouldn't wash. Hell, Pete was so old himself that all his uncles must have been killed in the war of 1812!"

Magpie grinned, "I thought Pete would think up a better one than that."

"Even mother saw through it, I guess, but she didn't ask too much because she was thinking about me. If she had really known, I expect she would have felt compelled to refuse. Not that anybody ought to mind your killin' Beasley. The old skinflint was much too crooked to live anyhow."

And suddenly Magpie's mind was filled with pictures he had half-forgotten....

HE HAD been with Martha Long that day at the bank, after Buff Long's death, when Beasley had showed her papers that she didn't know existed, and told her that the bank was taking her spread away from her. Magpie had been there because Buff Long was his old partner and it was his duty to help Martha anyway he could. At least that's the way it had been to everybody but Magpie, because nobody but Magpie knew that he had loved Martha Long for as long a time as Buff had.

Magpie knew as well as Martha did that there was something crooked about those papers. But there wasn't anyway to prove it.

He had been with Martha, too, when she'd told the kid... and that was worse. The kid had taken it tough. His chin had quivered just once, and just for a moment there had been something like terror in his eyes. Then that was gone and he was saying: "Shucks, mom, don't you mind. We'll get it some day. We can wait." Comforting her!

Magpie had known then what he had to do.

What followed was the bank hold-up and old Beasley blowing his top at the sight of his bank's money in Magpie's hand. He had rushed Magpie like a madman, at the last.

Magpie had fired a shot over his head to stop him, but the man was a maniac by then and he had come on, ripping the mask off Magpie's face. Magpie had knocked Beasley aside and then his nephew, the cashier, had grabbed a gun from behind the counter, and....

"Look, kid," Magpie said, "I reckon you won't believe me, but I got to tell you on the chance that it'll make you feel better about havin' used the money. I didn't kill Beasley. That nephew of his did it—shot him in the head in cold blood an' then tried to get me. I was jumping for the door, and he missed."

Dave Long's eyes blazed with excitement. "Hold on now. Hold on now. Tell me that again. That's important, because they've got that old charge against you, too."

Magpie shook his head. "I got no proof whatever. They wouldn't believe it."

Dave Long sat down on the bunk beside him. "No," he admitted. "They wouldn't believe it. The nephew owns the bank now—and the town."

Magpie put a hand on his shoulder. "Don't bother about it, younker," he said. "I didn't get you down here to be my lawyer. I just wanted to let you know that—seein' the fix I'm in—I wouldn't be able to help you out like you asked me to."

Dave Long stared. "Like—like I *asked* you to?"

"Why shore. In your letter."

"Letter? What letter?"

"You mean you didn't send me any letter?"

"Why, no. Lord knows I would have, if I had known where you were, but—"

Magpie was suddenly on his feet, limping excitedly about the cell. "Hell," he muttered. "This is bad. This is worse than I thought it was!"

113

HIS MIND was beginning to click how. The thing had been a frame-up from the beginning! Somebody, somehow, had found out about Magpie's relationship to Dave Long and had used it to pull him in here. Who—and why?

"Who knows about me sendin' you that money?" he asked.

Dave Long shrugged. "God knows. I've told half a dozen people myself, some years ago. It's a story that's known."

Then it might be anybody, Magpie thought. He sat down suddenly and told Dave Long what had happened this night—how he had been hit on the head, had waked up to find the stage robbed, and Silver Trent's gang accused.

"You're sure Trent had nothing to do with it?" Dave asked quickly.

"Hell, yes, I'm sure," Magpie flared.

"Why, then," Dave said promptly, "there's some other gang using Trent as a cover. This isn't the first time you know. There have been several robberies and killings around here recently. One especially bad one, of Harry Briscoe—a man everybody loved and respected. He was found bound and gagged and shot through the forehead at close range. Cold-blooded murder. And the town believes *that* was Silver Trent's work, too.

There was no evidence to connect the Trent gang with that particular robbery and killing, but there was in another—so everybody believes the same gang is responsible. And this thing tonight will clinch in everybody's mind!"

So that was it! Some other gang, trying to protect themselves against suspicion. But going to the length of pulling him,

Magpie, in here—hell, that was complicated. He didn't know anybody but Esteban Bautista—

Then it hit him like a blow between the eyes. That voice he had heard was Lobo Obrien's! Bautista's man. He was a fool not to have recognized it before; would have, likely, if his head had been right. It was Bautista who had lured him to Tucson and framed him. Bautista—El Diablo! He had been profiting from a few robberies and throwing the blame on Silver, but the robbery profits were secondary.

He was really setting the stage to get Silver hanged—to work the town up to a faring lynching madness and then bait Silver into the trap. Using Magpie as the bait. Hell! The whole gang would be lynched—as many as Silver brought in.

Magpie sat down again, his leathery brow furrowed. It was getting worse all the time! For naturally Silver and the rest would come the minute he heard Magpie was in jail—El Diablo would see that he heard of it, if nobody else did. Silver would think that all they had was the reasonably tough job of cracking a hard jail. And they'd run into a hornets' nest such as even they had never known. It would be a miracle if any one of them got out of it alive!

MAGPIE SAID feverishly, "I got to get a message to Silver. You know anybody I can trust to carry it? Ought to be some Mex, I think. You know one—a good one?"

Dave Long came out of a deep abstraction. "Hey? Oh! Why—why yes. I know one—Pedro Juarez."

"Get him. No, wait. Give me a pencil an' some paper."

He wrote, frowning for some minutes, then handed the paper

115

to Dave Long. 'Find your Pedro Juarez, son, an' get him started pronto. I've wrote directions for findin' the hideout after he gets to La Hoya."

Dave got up, nodding. "I'll start him tonight, and I'll see you tomorrow. We've got to talk more, after I've had a chance to think." He looked worried.

Magpie knew that Dave Long was thinking not only of a court trial. He was thinking that when the news got around tomorrow there was liable to be something a lot faster and deadlier than a trial. Now that Silver was to be warned, Magpie felt better. Silver was a tough man to beat when he knew what he was up against....

Next day, the body of a Mexican was found dead in a ditch by the road to Nogales and Mexico. The authorities were busy, and because it was only a Mexican, it was several days before the body was identified as that of one Pedro Juarez. The motive, they thought, must have been robbery, for there was nothing in his pockets....

CHAPTER 3
HURRY CALL
FOR HELL'S HAWKS

A WEEK later half a dozen men made a dark and dry camp in the Tuscon hills, to the northwest of the town. The forage there was poor, but the walls were high and cut them off from sight, as well as muffling the sounds of their horses—the snorting and stomping of tired animals trying to fill their bellies with sparse graze before they settled to rest.

The men squatted down in the dark, drinking cold coffee and eating cold beans and tortillas. The sound of their voices barely carried across the short space between them.

After they had eaten they lolled around smoking cigarettes.

"I don't know as I could think of any food like a cold tortilla," one of them said reflectively, "unless maybe it would be a section of paw's red flannels after they had hung out in a foggy winter night."

Somebody else made a sympathetic sound. "Bill shore must have had a thin boyhood," he remarked. "I bet his old man give him hell for eatin' them drawers."

Soundless laughter ran through the group.

"*Por Dios!*" another voice said. "My belly is still so empty that I would be tempted by some red flannel myself. To think that if Seelver had not become suddenly a seer of ghosts, we could be this minute with the wine and the girls in Tucson."

"*Carrao, si!* You think maybe Seelver is getting too soft for this work?"

Silver Trent finished rolling a smoke with one hand and lit the twisted end. The brief flare of the match in his cupped hands showed a look of wry amusement on his square-cut, hard face.

"To tell the truth," he murmured, "I don't know myself why I'm bein' so careful on this job. Hunch, maybe."

That was opening enough for the others. They ganged him like grinning wolves.

"Our Seelver, he becomes w'at you call spooky, eh?"

"Yeah, an' a fortune teller, at that!"

"Oh, dear Meester, I read in tea leaves that prett' soon you meet wit' nice dark man—"

Silver teeth flashed in the dim starlight. "All right, all right," he cut in. "Just the same, somethin' smells a leetle high about this.

"Magpie gets a letter an' goes to Tuscon, an' right away he's in jail for murder and stage robbery. Wasn't any need for him to pull a stage robbery, and it don't sound to me like he did. Magpie's not the man to botch a job with two killin's. It don't add up, and when things don't add right, I like to move in on 'em slow."

He sat thoughtful a moment, then said, "Ricardo, your horse has had some rest now. Ride in an' see what you can find out."

Ricardo murmured, "*Si,*" and got to his feet. There was an odd smoothness to the motion that made it appear almost slow—a deception to the eye which had cost more than one man dear. His walk as he moved toward his horse had the same feral grace in it.

When he was gone, Silver said to the others," Better roll up and get a couple of hours sleep. You might need 'em. I'll keep watch."

Within less than five minutes the deepened breathing of the others told him that they had had no difficulty in following his advice. He lay on his back and watched the great march of the stars across the ravine top....

HOW MANY nights, he wondered, had he lain so, shut off from the ways and comforts of ordinary men, lonely under that glittering and impersonal parade-up there? Too many. Perhaps they had all known too many such nights.

Sometimes he thought that he did his men no favor by hold-ing them together in his small, compact comradeship along the dim trails that must lead in the end to prison or sudden death. If it weren't for him, the gang might break up, scatter, find its individual ways back to some kind of respectability and safety.

Yet he knew that so far as he himself was concerned, he would not quit as long as Esteban Bautista lived. Some day, Silver thought, his bullets would send his distorted evil soul back to the Hell from which it must have sprung. When that happened, northern Mexico would be a cleaner and decenter place to live in.

Yet, for ten years his fight had run against Bautista El Diablo, as the humbler Mexicans called him. Ten years of constant, wearing battle against the odds of wealth and power and a ruth-lessness which was hampered by no rules of decency or kindness or honesty.

It was ironic that he—Silver Trent, the outlaw—lived by a code of decency which was as rigid as that of any man within the law, while Bautista, who hid behind the protection of that law, was more cruel and corrupt than any outlaw Trent had ever known.

By the same token more subtle and dangerous too....

Silver's mind drifted back to that old time when Bautista had murdered Silver's best friend and that friend's wife, in cold blood, to make the beginning of his power and fortune. Silver had shot him then, as he thought, to death. But despite the six slugs slamming into the man's body, Bautista lived on, with his body crippled and twisted by Silver's slugs, his heart seething with implacable hatred.

No, as long as Bautista lived to oppress decent people with his crooked power and trample on those who dared oppose him, so long would Silver carry on the fight against him. When El Diablo was dead.... Silver grinned faintly....

A wolf-lean figure lifted from among the sleeping men and drifted silently over to sit by Silver.

"You don't sleep, old one?" Silver asked.

"Not sleepy," Pablo answered curtly.

Silver grinned in the starlight. "You fight with Magpie like a bobcat would a hound dog, but you can't sleep until he is out of jail."

Pablo snorted uncomfortably. "Why should I worry about an old fool who can't keep out of trouble?"

"I wonder how many times you've saved his life at the risk of your own," Silver taunted him softly. "Or he yours."

"A man does not save his life except with the consent of the saints," Pablo replied piously.

"Those saints of yours must be pretty good natured," Silver prodded him. "Seems to me your conduct puts quite a burden on them."

"A man must have faith," Pablo said. "Without faith, he is nothing. Perhaps even God would be nothing, unless men had faith in him. The saints know this. Therefore they pardon all to the faithful."

TRENT'S EYES danced. He never got over his delight in the primitive and naive logic with which old Pablo reconciled his career and his piety—the fact that he always went into battle yelling curses which would have made the Devil himself blanch, yet maintained his confident belief that he was a favored servant of the hierarchy of heaven.

Maybe it wasn't so illogical at that, Silver reflected. You'd go far to meet a better friend, or a better man.

There was an almost inaudible noise of hoofbeats and Silver came to his feet fast and ghosted toward the entrance.

A moment or so later, Ricardo appeared out of the darkness. From the condition of his horse, he had ridden hard.

"It is bad, *Jefe,*" he breathed. "The trial is for tomorrow, and there is talk of a lynching. The jail is heavily guarded, because of the lynch talk. But my cousin says that it is sure that Magpie will be lynched anyway, as soon as the trial is over."

Rapidly, he outlined all that had taken place—the other robberies and killings and the fact that the Trent gang was blamed for them all.

Silver cursed, sudden rage hardening his face. "I'll find out who we have to thank for that," he said, and his tone was deadly, "and when I do...."

"*Jefe,* there is one other thing. Bautista is in town."

Silver stiffened, his eyes glacier cold and narrowed. "How long's he been in town?"

"My cousin didn't know. Maybe a month. He is said to be here to buy land for a ranchero. He spends much time with important men and also in gambling."

Silver drew a long breath. Bautista! It didn't take much sharpness to see who was behind all this now.

121

He stood for a long moment silent, shoving his hat back in the automatic gesture he had when he was thinking. Starlight shone faintly on the single lock of silvery hair which ran back diagonally from his forehead, which had given him his nickname.

Then he moved abruptly. "We'll have to make it tonight, and we've got to be careful. Come on."

Ricardo nodded, following him to wake the others. He did not mention his cousin's insistence that it would be suicide to try to crack the jail when it was so heavily guarded.

Half an hour later, they were at the outskirts of the darkened, sleeping town.

RICARDO LED them by alleys and narrow ways through the Mexican quarter until they came to a low shed under which they could leave their horses.

Silver murmured, "Lars, you stay with the horses."

Lars Johanssen stiffened. "Haal, Silver," he protested, "them hosses'll be all right here. Yah! Me, I—"

"We'll be coming back on foot an' maybe split up," Silver told him. "I need somebody here that will not only keep the horses safe, but can stand off anybody that gets here before we do. I can only spare one man for it, and it's got to be you."

The truculance went out of the big Scandinavian. He said, "Yah, su-ure," greatly soothed by the implied flattery.

Silver's mouth had the shadow of a smile as he turned and gave direction to the others.

Lars was too big, too easily recognizable for a job like this. And his temper was too unpredictable. At the first hint of opposition he was liable to wade in roaring, quite deaf to any order to retreat.

For Lars had been shot to ribbons and near death more than once, but the firm belief still persisted in him that he was impervious to bullets.

The gang split up, each man drifting off alone. Silver and Ricardo took the most direct route to the jail, walking over to the next street and down it, moving easily but covering ground fast.

Silver could feel the cold hammering begin in the pit of his stomach. His skin felt stretched and tight, with the nerve ends close to the surface, so that he felt the rub of his clothes.

It was always that way when he was shoving his crowd into danger. He couldn't rid himself of the nervous weight of his own responsibility.

Deep inside his head all the ways that disaster might strike were milling about. But above that was a cool layer of thought that dealt with actualities and the plans he had made.

A man was siting on a box in the shadow of the board fence beside the street on which stood the jail building. The fence ran along the street to the rear of the building ahead.

Silver saw that much from the shadow of a cottonwood, before the man saw him. He and Ricardo faded back behind the tree. A gesture held Ricardo in place, while Silver eased back up the street and came on again, walking on the board walk this time and singing tunelessly to himself. When he staggered out to the entrance to the jail alley, he paused a moment, then stumbled aimlessly toward the man, pretending not to see him. THE MAN got to his feet and Silver saw that he held a sawed-off shotgun in his hands. He didn't look suspicious but his manner was wary, just the same.

Silver stared at him stupidly. "Wha'?" he mumbled, "You, too?" And grimaced with uncoordinated, twitchy grin of the paralyzed drunk.

"You sure took on a package," the guard said, his wariness relaxing. "All right, move along. I ain't hankerin' fer comp'ny."

Under the pulled down brim of his hat, Silver's eyes had been searching the street but it appeared empty. He swayed toward the guard, stumbling a step towards him.

The man was grinning. "Beat it," he said, "I—"

He broke off sharp as Silver's right fist took him fairly on the point of the jaw. He slumped forward, and Silver caught him, easing him to the ground.

Swiftly he made a gag of the man's bandanna, bound his ankles with his belt and his wrists with cord with which he himself carried for that purpose. Then he and Ricardo dragged the unconscious guard to a clump of high weeds between the street and walk. While Ricardo took the guard's place, Silver drifted silently down until he was opposite the jail.

Two guards were at the entrance, one lolling back against the wall, the other seated on the step. Through the open door, Silver could see two men inside in the lighted jail office.

One of the outside guards yawned and complained, "Hell, I don't see what's got into Bill, keepin' us here this-a-way. Shucks, the boys has forgot about the lynchin'. They might get stirred up tomorrow at the trial, but not before. An' what the hell does Bill care anyhow, if they do lynch him?"

The other man twisted the end of a quirley and said, "I been wonderin' about that myself. Today, I got onto the reason for it. Bill don't want no lynchin' on his record, but he wouldn't shoot nobody to stop it. All this guarding is for two reasons—bluff an' trap. He aims to bluff the boys in town out of their lynchin' so's he can set a trap for the Trent gang. Feller named Bautista tipped him off that the gang would try to crack Myers out of jail. Bill wants 'em to try it."

"Who's Bautista?"

"Some rich greaser or breed from below the Border. He says they know Trent well down there, an' have been layin' for him. He's so shore the Trent gang will show up an' so pantin' to catch 'em that he's done got some of his vaqueros up here to help out."

"Vaqueros!" the first man said scornfully. "That's a hell of a name to call a cowpoke. An' a hell of a lot of good they'll be! Them durn Mex ain't good fer nothin' but herdin' sheep."

"Some of 'em can be kind of tough," the other one said mildly. "You live down in this country as long as I have an' you'll find out."

CHAPTER 4
ONE FOR ALL
AND ALL FOR ONE!

S ILVER HAD been watching a dim figure which was half silhouetted against the other end of the street, the jail being in the middle of the block. Doubtless, it was another guard. He waited, watching.

The end of the street was faintly lighted and after a moment he saw a figure he recognized stroll by, glance at the man in the shadows, salute carelessly and stroll on.

A moment later, the guard emerged from the shadow, going quickly toward the street. As he came level with it, an arm shot out from the corner building and the guard disappeared, jerked out of sight.

Within thirty seconds he was apparently back, with his gun, in the shadows.

Silver made his way back to Ricardo and murmured, "All right." He then returned to his former place, crouching behind the weeds.

Ricardo went into the street and walked toward the jail rapidly, like a man on urgent business.

At the jail entrance he took off his hat humbly and bowed to the two guards. *"Buena sera, señores.* Please, I mus' spik wis Señor Barclay. Is ver' *importante."* He sounded breathless.

"He's home asleep, hombre. You'll have to wait until tomorrow."

"Is mos' *importante,* señor," Ricardo repeated excitedly. "Is somesing about this Señor Myers—*el bandido.* I have *prueba*—what you say, proof? *Muy importante."*

The other guard spoke up. "Beat it, greaser. This case don't need no more proof."

Ricardo spread his hands. "Excuse, *Señor*—"

"Wait a minute," a voice from inside the office said curtly. "Don't any case have too much proof. Send him in, I'll talk to him."

126

Ricardo went in quickly.

Down at the other end of the street, the guard detached himself from the shadows and began to walk down toward the jail. The two at the door had their heads turned inward, listening to the Mexican.

Silver slid soundlessly to the edge of the lot. The guard came on and scuffed his foot. The two at the door turned their heads toward him, saw it was one of their own men, and turned back to the scene inside.

Silver grinned faintly, thinking that Ricardo must be making quite a story of it. In the instant when both guards had turned to look at their pardner, he had slipped across the road like a shadow. There wasn't much danger in that, because the oncoming "guard" was Bill Lang.

Inside, Ricardo was leaning forward in his chair and gesturing dramatically. "And so, *señores,*" he was saying, his eyes grown large with excitement, "my cousin, he tell me about—"

There was the sound of a sharp crack, a smothered exclamation and the slump of a body from the doorway. The deputy and the jailer whirled in the direction of the sound and jerked to their feet.

A MAN stood there with a gun in his hand. He was big, with wide, powerful shoulders which sloped down to make almost a V at his waist. His square-cut weathered features were set hard just now and his eyes, dark gray in the lamplight, looked like glacier ice at the close of a winter day.

His voice, when he spoke, had the same, temperature. "Don't make any noise or any bad moves," he warned.

Ricardo slid forward and took the deputy's gun. The jailer wasn't armed.

Silver walked in, with Bill Lang behind him, while two other men, Mexicans, appeared and began to drag the two guards.

"You can give me the key to Myers' cell while you're alive," Silver said coldly, "or you can make me look for it on corpses."

A knife flicked into Ricardo's hand and the point of it tickled the deputy's throat. "The killing will be quiet, amigo," he said softly.

The deputy's face went white. He knew this for the Trent gang and it was plain that the terror of their reputation chilled his stomach.

"I—I haven't got it. Bill Barclay, the marshal—he took it, just on this account. If a mob come or—or you."

His voice didn't reflect the fear of his face, but it sounded true.

Silver swore softly. "We'll have to saw the bars then. Tie and gag all four of them and put them in one of the other cells. Then, Bill you go on back an' be guard again. Juan and Paco will sit outside. Wear the hats of the Americanos, amigos."

He slid a small business-like saw out from under his shirt and strode toward the cells, Pablo following him with a bunch of keys to try in case the deputy had lied.

In the cell, Magpie was awake, grinning at them.

"Son, it's shore agreeable to see you. This durn old neck of mine was already beginnin' to be stretched out of shape, jest, thinkin' about it."

"You're a liar," Silver grinned back. "You figured we'd be here."

He got out the saw and went to work. The cell bars were set in cement and they were hard, heavy steel. He didn't let it show in his manner but he knew that not getting the key was bad luck. It would take time to saw through these bars, and from the smell of this trap they might not have any time.

Pablo was insulting Magpie with satisfaction. "When the fox is old, his claws are dull and his teeth blunt. Also his nose—"

Outside, Juan's voice said softly. "One comes, in a hurry, *Jefe*."

"Go see, Pablo." Silver continued to saw.

"You—you hadn't ought to have tried this, Silver," Magpie said reluctantly.

Outside, there was a quick exchange of talk and Pablo came in prodding Dave Long ahead of him. "He says he is Magpie's *abogado*," he announced curtly.

DAVE LONG took in the situation and began to protest. He seemed excited. "You can't get away with this," he said quickly. "Barkley has somebody come around and inspect the guards and the jail every fifteen minutes or so. There are two dozen men in a building across the way, sleeping with their clothes on. You're going to ruin everything, both for yourselves and for Magpie."

"Silver smiled at him faintly. "Don't get excited, amigo. We'll make out."

From outside began a faint pounding sound that seemed to come from somewhere up the street.

Silver cursed suddenly. He had a quick guess as to what it was. The man he had tied up had come to life and managed to roll over to the fence. He was pounding on it with both heels.

"Listen, Magpie," Dave Long's voice was urgent. "Don't do

this. I—I think I can get you out of this. I've got a good chance. Send your friends away, at least until after the trial."

Magpie shook his head impatiently. "You got a chance, but this is sure."

"Listen," Dave Long said desperately. "You can be free—free of all charges, maybe. You know what that would mean to mother and me. And, by God, if they convict you, I'll help you escape myself!"

Juan came in, breathing fast. *"Jefe,* somebody was pounding on the fence. I went down to stop him, but a crowd came around the corner. I couldn't stop them without shooting."

Silver said curtly, "Go get Bill, an'—"

But Bill was already at the door. His voice was taut. "Crowd formin' at the square corner, Silver. Heard 'em say jail."

Silver kept the saw moving. "We can hold 'em off," he snapped. "Shut the office door and fort up."

"Wait a minute!" Magpie's voice was suddenly hard. "I've changed my mind, boys. I ain't goin'. Dave here has got a right to his chance to get me off. An'—an' by God, I want it. I'm tired of bein' hunted. I want a chanct to be peaceful in my old age."

Silver straightened up, leaving the saw in bar half sawn through. He stared at Magpie. "You're lyin', you old coot."

"No I'm not," Magpie said stubbornly.

"I ain't goin'." He snatched the saw from the bar and tossed it onto his bunk.

Silver swore in a flat monotone. "What are the ways out of here?" he snapped.

"Front door—side door at your right—an' a trap door to the roof," Magpie said crisply.

A voice outside yelled, "Open up in there, an' come out with your hands up. We got you surrounded."

"Trap door," Silver snapped. "Come on."

Paco, his ugly, pockmarked face taut, said, "I looked out the window. There must be twenty of them out there. Most of them Bautista men, I think, but some from this town."

Ricardo swarmed up Silver's back. The trap door was padlocked on the inside. Ricardo pulled his gun and tapped the lock expertly with the barrel, springing it open. The trap door raised without sound and Ricardo disappeared.

Outside, at the front door, a sixgun slammed twice, the slugs hammering at the lock of the front door. An instant later, three more shots sounded at the side door.

One after another, moving swiftly and soundlessly, the other four were helped up by Silver and disappeared through the trap. Silver jumped. His hooked steel fingers caught the edge of the door-frame and he pulled himself up.

Below, the door burst in, then there was a moment of silence. He knew that the posse was staring suspiciously at the lighted emptiness of the office.

"All right," a voice snapped. "Rush 'em!"

FEET SLAMMED on the office floor. Once the rush was started, it sounded like the whole gang had crowded in. Silver smiled thinly. Somebody had more sense than courage. He thought of what they could have done to a rush like that from the darkened cell block.

He led the way to the edge of the roof away from the side door. Only two men were in sight.

One was standing with a shotgun by the corner of the nearest shop. Another was making his way cautiously along the building toward the rear. Silver saw that the side of the shop connected with a high 'dobe wall which formed the side and rear of the jail yard.

He jumped, his knees catching the man below on the shoulders, driving his face to the dust. The man at the corner flung up his shotgun at Silver's first movement, as a hunter does when a partridge breaks cover. But the shotgun never went off. Pablo's shot hit the man's shoulder, spinning him hard.

Silver hit his man behind the ear and led the way to the 'dobe wall.

One by one, the others hit his cupped hand and went over, as half a dozen men began to boil out from the rear of the building. Inside, there was yelling and confusion, as the posse realized what had happened and broke for the doors.

While he held one hand cupped, Silver shot with the other. A man at the rear went down with a smashed thigh. Another howled and grabbed his gunarm. The others shot more or less wildly and then dived for the cover of the corner of the building.

Ricardo, the last of the five, hit Silver's hand and went up like a bird. On top of the wall, he turned, reaching his hands down to Silver.

A man jumped around the front corner of the jail. He went down under an instant shot from Pablo, who was hanging by one arm to the wall with his body on the other side.

A man shot from the corner at the rear as Silver jumped. The bullet slapped into the wall at his side. Paco and Juan, hanging like Pablo, opened up. Lead seared along Silver's shoulder as he hit the top of the wall and went over. A sawed-off shotgun blasted and a double charge of buckshot whistled over Silver's head as he dropped. Then they were running, under cover.

BEFORE THE jail, Bill Barkley slammed the empty scattergun to the ground. "What are you standin' around for?" He bellowed. "Get after 'em!" He spat orders, his voice exploding like a bunch of firecrackers.

A thin twisted figure in black held up a hand. "Never mind, men," he said sharply. Three quarters of the crowd stopped in their tracks.

The marshal whirled on him. "Who in hell are you to give orders around here?"

"You might as well try to follow Apaches in the dark," the man in black said bitterly. "You've bungled it. Your accursed stupid guards—"

"Shut up!" The marshal thrust a purpled, menacing face at him. "I'm not takin' any talk like that from a greaser. You—"

"Greaser?" The dark man's voice was as soft as the slither of a snake on leaves.

The marshal's speech broke off, and he glared furiously into a pair of dark, narrowed eyes that had something almost hypnotic in their icy venom.

The marshal swallowed. He was aware that all around him Mexican faces were turned toward him stonily and that hands had stolen to guns. It came to him with a shock that these vaqueros who rode for Señor Esteban Bautista were tougher men than he had thought. They looked now like a crowd of hungry wolves.

He said, "All right—all right, Bautista. I talked out of turn. No use in us squabblin' about it. You're right about my damn guards bein' no good. By God, somebody's goin' to pay for this."

Bautista was no longer listening. The venomous eyes in the vulturine face had grown veiled and scheming, yet without, somehow, losing their viciousness.

The marshal's eye caught sight of Dave Long standing in the doorway of the jail and his anger came back with a rush.

"By God, you're responsible for this, Long," he yelled. He surged forward and swung at the lawyer. The blow hit Dave in the chest as he tried to dodge and knocked him backward. "You'll rot in jail before I get through with you."

He was advancing as he spoke. Dave Long picked up a heavy glass paperweight from the desk. "Come any farther and I'll knock your head off, Barkley," the kid snapped, grim-faced. "I didn't help with this jail break. I came in time to keep Myers from going out—an' to keep a lot of you from being killed."

"He's right, I reckon, Bill," the deputy said. "I was tied up in that cell, but I could hear. He persuaded Myers not to go along."

"Smooth, ain't you? Well, I ain't satisfied. You stay here until I get a chance to look into this."

Dave Long sat down in a chair by the desk.

The office had been quietly torn apart by Silver's men looking for the key to the cell door. The desk was almost completely wrecked. Idly Dave Long glanced at the jumbled contents of the big, opened drawer. There was a belt with twin guns, a clasp knife, a ball of cord, a worn wallet, some change in silver, and a gold, hunting case watch. They were Magpie's things. He had checked them briefly the day after Magpie had been arrested.

The hunting case watch was dented. He reached down and picked it up. The dent was in the back of the watch and it was deep, deep enough likely to ruin the works. Dave figured it must have been made by a sharp rock when Magpie fell. He opened the front of the watch and saw that the face had bulged out, cracking the glass. It was ruined, no doubt about that.

"Hey, you—what are you doin'? Put that watch down."

Dave Long put the watch back in the drawer and stood up. There was a queer, intent look in his eye. "I don't like your manner, Barkley," he said quietly. "If you want to talk to me, do it tomorrow—when you've cooled down."

He turned on his heel and walked out.

CHAPTER 5
HELL-TOWN TRIAL

THE COURT house was on the second floor of the 'dobe building and it was jammed long before the session opened. A mixed crowd—townsmen, ranchers, cowboys from the surrounding range, a sprinkling of Mexicans had shoved in with the jam, even a few women.

The atmosphere was tense, grim—the murmur of talk low-pitched. A few of the Mexicans looked excited and happy, like children before a play. One of them in particular—an ugly,

135

pockmarked man—was wide-eyed, rapt, fairly lost in delighted anticipation. A simple man, evidently; naive and childish.

In the aisle against the back wall, another Mexican squatted, swathed in a serape and with a tall straw sombrero pulled over his eyes. His face, or what could be seen of it, looked lean and weathered, with the cheeks hollow and drawn. His shoulders looked hunched, somehow crippled under the serape. A corn-husk cigarette, partly smoked and unlighted, drooped from his lips. He appeared absorbed in picking at the toes of a pair of brown, bare and very dirty feet.

A sharp observer might have noted, even in his squatting position, that he was unusually large and big-boned for a Mexican.

Several seats away from him near a window, sat a man with blue eyes and a heavy drooping mustache. His cheeks were plump and he had a paunch, yet his shoulders looked almost lean and there was a granite jut to his chin.

Outside in the hall, where part of the overflow crowd had gathered, there was a momentary disturbance and some audible grumbling, then a twisted man, dressed in fine black broadcloth, pushed through and took a seat which had been reserved for him near the prosecuting attorney's table.

He wore an expensive black Stetson, which he did not remove at once. Under it, his black, curiously malevolent eyes ran swiftly about the room, looking over the crowd.

Somebody in front of the big Mexican who was picking his toes said: "There's that rich Mex, Bautista, who was helpin' to trap the Trent gang."

The big Mexican heard it clearly because his cigarette had fallen out of his mouth and he was leaning forward to pick it up. When he resumed his former posture he had shifted somehow so that the man in front of him was between him and Señor Bautista.

The outer door opened again, letting in the prosecutor and, at the same time, the murmur of the overflow crowd which filled the hall and cluttered the stairs.

A moment later a door in the back of the room opened and four deputies armed with shotguns came through. Behind them, was the prisoner, Magpie Myers, with the town marshal and his deputy. Magpie was handcuffed to the deputy.

An ugly growl ran through the room at the sight of him—a growl which was cut short by the pounding of the judge's gavel who came in from his office then.

The jury was already in place, and the trial began.

IT WENT fast. The prosecution called only six witnesses: Marshal Bill Barkley, his deputy, the drummer who had been in the coach, a townsman, the president of a bank in the nearby town of Counterpane named Beasley, and an old timer from the same town.

Barkley told his story of finding Magpie, wounded and unconscious, at the scene of the holdup. And recounted also the attempt by the Trent gang to get him out of jail the night before. He also testified to other robberies and affirmed his belief that all had been the work of the Trent gang, of which Magpie was a member.

The deputy did little more than corroborate his testimony.

The drummer recounted his experience in the coach alleging that he had been helpless because unarmed, else he might have "gotten a few of 'em, myself."

A snicker drifted through the courtroom at this and the drummer flushed. He also told of hearing Silver's name called during the holdup and Silver's answer.

The Tucson townsman followed, testifying that he had been within hearing distance of the gang when they left after the earlier robbery and murder of Harry Briscoe, and had also heard Silver's name called.

The banker, Beasley, next took the stand. He was a short, plump individual, with a smooth face and pale, cold looking eyes behind gold-rimmed glasses.

The prosecutor addressed him with every mark of respect. After recognizing the defendant, Beasley said he last saw him in the act of robbing the Beasley Bank and "shot and killed my uncle, Josiah Beasley."

A heavy murmur, like a composite snarl, ran through the courtroom, and the judge rapped for order. The testimony had been expected, but the effect was apparently just as great as though it had come as a surprise.

The smooth, plumb witness then went on to recount the details of the fifteen-year-old robbery. His fellow townsman, following him, testified that he had run a store opposite the bank and had seen Magpie, whom he knew, race out of there just after the shooting, with a canvas sack in his hand, jump on his horse, and ride away.

The defense rested, looking openly triumphant.

The big Mexican against the wall narrowed eyes which were startlingly gray for one of his race. Magpie's lawyer didn't seem to be doing so good. He had sat abstractedly, making aimless marks on a sheet of paper before him during all the testimony.

The only times he had spoken had been when the prosecutor had finished examining a witness and had said, "Your witness." At such times, Dave Long had shaken his head indifferently and said, "No cross examination."

Then Dave Long got to his feet.

"GENTLEMEN," HE said, addressing the jury, "you have listened to what seems to be that rare thing—a perfect case. And you are going to have an interesting experience. You are going to see that case torn to pieces. You are going to see that my client is the victim of one of the most elaborate frame-ups it has ever been your experience to encounter. And at the end of it, in justice and right, as is your duty, you are going to declare him not guilty and permit him to walk out of this court a free man."

A gasp ran through the courtroom, but the faces which leaned forward in renewed interest were still hard and skeptical.

As a first witness, to the obvious surprise of the court, Dave Long called Magpie to the stand. He took the witness chair still manacled to the deputy and was sworn in.

"Mr. Myers," Dave Long said respectfully, "will you tell the court and the jury just what happened to you on the night the Nogales coach was robbed."

Magpie told, simply and clearly, what had happened to him that night, from the time he had come to the roadhouse to the time he was hit on the head and waked to find himself under arrest.

Dave Long had Magpie step down and called a blond, rotund man who took the oath in a voice heavy with accent.

DAVE OPENED a box in front of him and took out Magpie's watch. "Mr. Zorich," he said, "you are something of an expert on watches, aren't you?"

"Ya. I vork twenty year als vatchmaker in Sweitzer before I come hier. Also hier in Tucson I fix many vatches many year." He grinned. "I t'ink efferbody hier knows dot."

Dave handed him the watch. "Will you look at this please, and tell the jury what you see."

The Swiss examined the watch attentively, making clucking, regretful sounds as he did so. "Dis iss a Sweitzer watch, very fine," he said looking up. "Vot a shame—vot a shame it iss ge-broken—smashed."

"What, in your opinion broke it?"

"I dunno. Maybe it is hit vit somet'ing. Maybe de mann who vear it fall on somet'ing—sharp rock, maybe."

"The hands stopped at a certain place did they not? Could they have been moved after the watch was smashed?"

The watchmaker shook his head. "De hands are shoved up against de cracked crystal. Also de set-wind is gebroken."

"Then the time you can read there now is the time when the watch was broken—fifteen minutes after nine?"

Dave Long whirled on the prosecutor, his eyes blazing. "Your witness," he snapped.

The attorney got up with his face red and began hastily

to cross-examine. He had evidently been caught by surprise though, and he did not make a good impression. The watchmaker stuck to his evidence.

Fast now, his voice going like a gatling gun, Dave Long recalled the marshal, deputy and passenger, establishing the time of the holdup fifteen minutes after Magpie's watch had stopped.

From the deputy he drew the reluctant admission that the hands had not been changed. They had read nine-fifteen that night when he had first seen the watch.

Also, Magpie had been lying on his face and the deputy remembered a sharp rock which was just under where his watch pocket might have been.

Cross examination only served to strengthen the evidence. The prosecutor sat down flustered.

Next, Dave called the doctor who had attended Magpie.

"In your opinion was the bruise on the head made before the bullet wound in the defendant's leg that you treated, or after it."

"Certainly before. The gunshot wound was very fresh—not more than fifteen minutes old, I estimate. The patient, I understand, had been conscious almost that long. In any case...."

The prosecutor was on his feet, his face red. "Conjecture—guess-work," he shouted.

Dave called the bartender of the road-house and one of the customers. Both testified that Magpie's watch was right at nine-ten.

He whirled on the jury. "There goes your case, gentlemen," he rapped out. "My client left the roadhouse at nine-ten. He had only time enough to get up to where he was hit on the head by nine-fifteen. His watch stopped when he fell on that rock. He was unconscious when found. Therefore he was unconscious during the stage robbery. Proven, point by point!

"Let me draw your attention to another fact. Do you believe for one moment that a gang of outlaws as experienced as the Trent gang would—*twice in succession*—make the same amateurish mistake of calling one another's names where they could be heard? Some other gang, gentlemen, is trying to use the Trent gang as a cover. The frame-up is too obvious to swallow. Take it another way, if you choose to believe that the Trent gang framed Myers, then why did it come here and try to get him out of jail—if it did? It won't wash gentlemen!

"But my job is not to clear the Trent gang. It's to clear my client—and that's what the plain evidence has done. Magpie Myers had no more to do with that holdup and robbery than you or I did!"

The prosecutor got to his feet. "I'd like to remind the counsellor that there are two charges of murder here.

"One murder was done fifteen years ago. Maybe he'd like to make out that the defendant has been a woolly white lamb since then, and anybody who believes that can stand on his head. But murder's murder and a cold-hearted murderer is a murderer, whether he killed fifteen years ago or fifteen minutes!"

CHAPTER 6
A FRIEND IN NEED

DAVE LONG turned to the jury and said, "Exactly. The learned prosecutor is right. There are two charges of murder. And with his honor's permission, I'd like to recall the defendant, to testify about that first murder charge."

Magpie took the stand again.

"Mr. Myers," Dave Long asked. "Why did you come to Tucson?"

"To see you. I had a letter signed with your name sayin' you was in a jam."

"Where is that letter?"

"It was took off me when I got knocked out. Leastways, I had it before, an' I didn't have it afterwards."

"Do you think I wrote the letter?"

"No. You said you didn't."

"Then the letter must have been written by somebody else, to lure you into Tucson at that time?"

The prosecutor was on his feet, red-faced. "I object, Your Honor. What Counsel thinks is immaterial."

The judge nodded.

Dave Long took a deep breath and smiled gently at the jury.

"Did you rob the bank in Counterpane fifteen years ago, Mr. Myers!"

"Yes." And Magpie looked acutely embarrassed when Dave Long asked him why.

"I wanted to help a friend that I thought had been cheated by the bank," Magpie said uncomfortably.

"Who was the friend you wanted to help, Mr. Myers?"

"It was your mother," Magpie said reddening. "I was your dad's old partner. After he died, your maw was going to lose the spread. Her an' I both thought the bank was cheatin' her. We didn't have any legal proof, but we both knowed it, because we had knowed your dad in the old days."

"So believing that, you took the law in your own hands?"

"Yeah."

"Was there a special reason why my mother needed money?"

"You was crippled," Magpie said irritably. "An operation would let you walk."

"Did you send the money, secretly, for that operation, after you had robbed the bank."

"Yeah." Magpie writhed visibly.

"And you put me through law school?"

"Shore."

"You can step down for the moment, Mr. Myers."

DAVE LONG was working fast now, his eyes glowing, his voice crisp, incisive. He called one Pete Sorenson to corroborate Magpie's testimony. Sorenson, it appeared, was the man who had delivered the money, saying that it was a legacy he had gotten.

Then Dave Long had himself sworn in. He corroborated getting the money from Sorenson. And he did an eloquent job of telling what it meant to a crippled kid to walk straight again.

"That," Dave Long ended, "is what I owe to that so-called murderer there."

Abruptly, his manner changed. "Take the stand again, Mr. Myers. How did you have to kill Josiah Beasley?"

"I didn't kill him," Magpie answered curtly. Then Magpie turned deliberately in his chair and pointed a gnarled finger. "His nephew—John Beasley killed him!"

A gasp ran through the courtroom. For an instant John Beasley's plump, prosperous form seemed to shrink in the chair and his pale face was white.

"An outrageous lie!" he roared.

"In that case," Dave Long said carelessly, "I wish to call Mr. Beasley as a defense witness!"

The effect was like a bombshell. The jury stared. The crowd gasped. Beasley—as a *defense* witness! And in the back of the room, the big Mexican swore softly and admiringly in excellent American.

DAVE LONG began, almost indifferently questioning Beasley. "Is it true that an attempt was made to rob your bank six months ago?"

Beasley's pale eyes flickered. "Why—er—yes." His pompous manner gave the impression that he couldn't see the point of the question.

"At that time your partner was killed, was he not?"

"Yes." Beasley's voice held deep regret. "Poor Charley was—"

The flick of Dave's voice brought color to the banker's face. "What happened to the robber?"

"He was killed. I had the good—"

Dave cut him off. "At the time of the death of your uncle, who inherited his estate?"

"Why—er—a good part of him came to me. Naturally I—?"

"Isn't it true that you were his only heir?"

"Since there were no other heirs you must have known or guessed that you would inherit everything he had then?"

"Why I—I hadn't ever thought about it."

DAVE LONG smiled scornfully. "Did you benefit financially from the death of your partner six months ago?" he asked abruptly.

"Your honor, I object—"

"Over-ruled."

"Exception." The prosecutor sat down, mopping his face with his handkerchief.

"Did you?" Dave's voice was sharp.

"Why not exactly. I—"

"Isn't it true that you had an agreement by which, in the case of the either of you dying before the other, the remaining partner would inherit the other's share in the bank?"

"Yes." Spots of angry color glowed in Beasley's cheeks. His pale eyes glittered. "That was to protect the depositors. The bank might have been weakened if—"

"Yes, yes, Mr. Beasley. But you are the sole owner of the bank now?"

"Yes." The admission was almost sullen.

Dave Long leaned forward. "Isn't it true," he thundered suddenly, "that you murdered both your uncle and your partner for the gain it would bring you, Beasley?"

"No! No! Of course it's not true. How dare you-"

Dave's voice lowered again; became tinged with deadly

menace. "Isn't it true that, like most murderers, you followed a pattern—killed the second time in the same way that had been successful the—"

"Objection, your honor!" roared the prosecutor. "The witness has—"

"Sustained."

Dave Long looked at John Beasley as though he were a beetle on a stick. "Step down." Then he turned about and said, "Call Pokey Nelson."

The witness came to the stand. When he was sworn, Dave Long asked, "Where do you work?"

"I swamp out the Beasley Bank in Counterpane." He looked nervously at John Beasley. But the banker was looking at Dave Long.

"You realize that you are under oath," Dave Long said quietly, "An' that you're bound to tell nothing but the truth?"

"Yes, suh." The witness grinned uncomfortably. "Seein' that I reckon I'm goin' to lose the only job I got, I wouldn't hardly lie to do it."

"Tell what you know about the bank robbery last April."

"I was comin' to swamp out. I stopped to look in at the side winder. I seen Mr. Corbin—him that was Mr. Beasley's partner—grab a gun an' shoot the robber. Then I seen Mr. Beasley shoot Mr. Corbin. But I ain't told anybody this before."

"No! You lyin' scum." Beasley jumped to his feet, his face maniacal as he turned to Dave Long. "*You're* responsible for this!" His hand flashed to his hip pocket, yanked out a short-barreled gun.

CHAPTER 7
EL DIABLO PLAYS HIS HAND

BEHIND HIM, a lean-faced Mexican with blazing fanatical eyes moved like a snake striking. The barrel of his six-gun, appearing from nowhere, cracked behind the banker's ear just before the short-barreled gun fired its bullet ploughing harmlessly into the ceiling.

Beasley slumped, dead to the world. The room was in an uproar of exclamation and cheering. Men pounded one another on the back. It was plain that they knew they had been witnesses to a trial that would go down in the history of Tucson.

It took minutes to restore order. But no more than one minute for the jury to decide on a verdict of not guilty on both counts against Magpie Myers.

The cheering broke out again. Dave Long grasped Magpie's hand. A dazed deputy put a key in the lock to take off Magpie's handcuffs.

Then a sharp, high, squawling voice cracked out. "Quiet! Quiet a minute." It was that twisted Mexican, Bautista. Heads turned toward the blazing malevolence of his voice. He stood on a chair, the black, doctor's bag clutched still in his left hand.

"One member of the Trent gang may have had his neck saved by a smart lawyer," he shouted, "but there's bigger game than that here. *Silver Trent* himself is in this court—with three of his gang!"

His long clawed fingers flung out, pointing to the big Mexican at the back of the room. "That's Trent—disguised as a Mexican! Get him!"

The big Mexican came to his feet fast. As he moved, his serape fell from his shoulders and a pair of sixguns were in his hands.

"Don't move, anybody," he snapped.

But a Bautista man had already moved. Leaning out from behind a townsman, he leveled his gun at Silver Trent, and shot.

Silver's gun had swung towards him at the first movement and the two shots sounded almost as one. The Bautista man slammed backward with a shocked grunt as lead slammed into his shoulder. Beside Silver's ear a Mexican's slug smacked into the wall.

Instantly the courtroom was bedlam, with spectators diving behind benches and chairs, or rushing for corners. A group nearest the door crowded for it, but the door opened inward and their weight jammed it shut.

By Magpie, the deputy and the marshal both had gone for their guns. Magpie, still manacled to the deputy, jumped out of his chair, "Look out!" he yelled as though scared and slammed into the deputy, knocking him into the marshal.

Barkley's gun was leveled at Silver, but he missed as the deputy knocked into him. Instantly, Silver's gun spoke again. The bullet hit the marshal's Colt, knocking it from his hand.

Cursing, struggling with Magpie, the deputy tried to get his gun into action. A bullet clipped his ear. "Drop it," a voice yelled, "or next time I'll put it in your thick skull!"

It was the lean-faced Mexican who had knocked Beasley out.

In the same instant, the pockmarked Mexican who had

watched the trial with so delighted an air, appeared on a bench with a sawed-off shotgun in his hand. He had dived forward to grab the gun at the first hint of trouble, had taken it from under the bench in front of him, where it had evidently been planted the night before.

Now he swung it at the dazed shotgun deputies who were just beginning hesitantly to lift their own guns.

"I got one too, hombres," he said. "Don' mak' me use eet." He did not look childish or naive any more.

Magpie was jerking at the deputy's wrist. "Git this durn iron off of me," he snapped.

Dave Long caught him by the arm urgently. "Quit it," he whispered. "They've got it under control. Don't get yourself in wrong again. Man, can't you see it? You're free now. Your outlaw days are over."

WHAT DAVE said looked true. Bill Lang, his cheeks, still artificially plumped out, and the false mustache still drooping from his lip, had taken up a place by the windows, a gun in each hand.

The room, acrid with the fumes of powdersmoke, had gone still.

"You can settle down now, Magpie—come and live with mother and me," Dave said.

The door where the crowd had jammed burst open suddenly, sending those against it tumbling over each other in a heap. A huge man with a chest like a barrel and blazing blue eyes strode in with a gun in each hamlike hand.

"Somebody vant fight?" he bellowed.

Silver grinned at him. "Too late now, old pardner," he said. "It's time to ride."

Lars turned to the crowd at his back which was trying to push in. They saw his guns and immediately were just as anxious to get back. "Back oop, you fallers," he roared. He shoved the door to with his foot. And then let out a tremendous howl like a wolf. "Bring 'em up, Ricardo," he yelled.

But there was already the stomp of hoofs below—outside the side windows.

Silver began to back toward the windows, his gray eyes cold, menacing. "Anybody that tries anythin' now will start a shambles," be warned.

The others began to move toward the window also. Below there would be guns but the men who carried them would still be a little bewildered. If Silver, and his crowd moved fast, they might get away without killing anybody.

"We'll both be proud to have you," Dave Long said to Magpie. "Why, shucks, you're goin' to be a kind of a hero around here, after this."

Magpie sat down a little weakly on the witness chair. He was thinking of peace in his old age; a girl he remembered....

His abstracted gaze fell on the twisted figure of El Diablo, his face was livid with rage, partly hidden behind a group of townsman in one corner.

"What kind of lawmen are you?" he cried out as the gang moved toward the window. "Are you going to let them get away."

Silver gave an order in a low voice and the others of the gang vaulted out of the window. One of the deputies moved and Silver's gun swung toward him.

"I told you to take it easy," he warned.

He swung one leg through the window, looked at Magpie. "So long, old timer," he said clearly, "Good luck!"

Magpie dropped his eyes. And then, for the first time he saw that the key had been left in the handcuffs. The deputy had been about to free him when all this had begun. It had only been seconds ago, though it seemed like hours.

He lifted burning eyes to Silver, "Hey, wait!" he yelled.

The cuff dangled loose and he was jumping like a white-haired scorpion toward the group behind which Bautista quickly hid.

They gave way before him, as before a madman. Bautista let out a strangled squawk and went for the gun he had been too wise to try to use before.

Magpie's left hand pinned the gun to his chest, while his right connected with a loud crack to Bautista's jaw. Bautista, better known as El Diablo, gave at the knees, and the gun came loose in Magpie's hand. In the same instant, he stooped and snatched the black bag from Bautista's grip. Then he was racing for the windows.

He whirled when he got there, gun on the crowd, and put one leg over as Silver had done. "So long, Dave," he said. "I owe you plenty, boy. And some day I'll be seeing you!"

Silver said, "Now!" and together they whirled and dropped.

There were sudden shouts from below and a quick hammer

of gunfire. Nobody in the room appeared in a hurry to get to the window.

Dave ran forward as the pound of hoofs began and new gunfire began to crackle. He was just in time to see them—all of them—whirl around a corner in a cloud of dust and disappear.

When he turned back to the courtroom his eyes were a little stunned. "Well I'll—be—damned!" he said softly.

What Esteban Bautista was saying, however, was a good deal stronger....

THEY HAD reached the foothills of the Quivaris before Silver pulled up to breathe the horses. There had been a pursuit of a kind, but it was too far behind to trouble them now that they had reached these hills.

Magpie handed the bag to Silver. "They still got my knife at the jail," he said. "You open her."

Silver ripped the bag open and saw that it was stuffed with greenbacks.

Silver shook his head. "It'll have to go back to the ones it was taken from," he said. "We'll do without money that has that much blood on it."

Ricardo groaned, but Magpie shrugged. "Better that way," he said. "Then they'll know it wasn't us. Say, some of those bills was marked, I heard. Look for red ink marks.

Silver had been counting the money. "Hey!" he exclaimed suddenly, "How much was taken in those robberies?"

"Forty-seven thousand dollars."

Silver grinned. "Bautista gambles pretty well. There's sixty-eight thousand here. I reckon we make a little profit."

Silver counted out forty-seven thousand dollars and handed the bills to Magpie. "You can take it back, old friend," he said. "It'll make even more of a hero of you. You'll collect the reward money, and with your share of this other and what you have salted away you'll be plenty well off. An' in the bargain, you'll ruin Bautista!"

Magpie grunted. "We can send it with a letter—and the bag. That'll make him an outlaw just the same."

Silver looked at him with the shadow of a smile about his lips. "It must be kind of hard to realize all at once," he said. "But we're a free man now."

"I realize it, all right," Magpie said grumpily. "I was realizin' it back in that court, after they acquitted me." He grinned suddenly. "It damn' near like to skeered me to death!"

THE SPIDER

❏ #1: The Spider Strikes — $13.95
❏ #2: The Wheel of Death — $13.95
❏ #3: Wings of the Black Death — $13.95
❏ #4: City of Flaming Shadows — $13.95
❏ #5: Empire of Doom! — $13.95
❏ #6: Citadel of Hell — $13.95
❏ #7: The Serpent of Destruction — $13.95
❏ #8: The Mad Horde — $13.95
❏ #9: Satan's Death Blast — $13.95
❏ #10: The Corpse Cargo — $13.95
❏ #11: Prince of the Red Looters — $13.95
❏ #12: Reign of the Silver Terror — $13.95
❏ #13: Builders of the Dark Empire — $13.95
❏ #14: Death's Crimson Juggernaut — $13.95
❏ #15: The Red Death Rain — $13.95
❏ #16: The City Destroyer — $13.95
❏ #17: The Pain Emperor — $13.95
❏ #18: The Flame Master — $13.95
❏ #19: Slaves of the Crime Master — $13.95
❏ #20: Reign of the Death Fiddler — $13.95
❏ #21: Hordes of the Red Butcher — $13.95
❏ #22: Dragon Lord of the Underworld — $13.95
❏ #23: Master of the Death-Madness — $13.95
❏ #24: King of the Red Killers — $13.95
❏ #25: Overlord of the Damned — $13.95
❏ #26: Death Reign of the Vampire King — $13.95
❏ #27: Emperor of the Yellow Death — $13.95
❏ #28: The Mayor of Hell — $13.95
❏ #29: Slaves of the Murder Syndicate — $13.95
❏ #30: Green Globes of Death — $13.95
❏ #31: The Cholera King — $13.95
❏ #32: Slaves of the Dragon — $13.95
❏ #33: Legions of Madness — $12.95
❏ #34: Laboratory of the Damned — $12.95
❏ #35: Satan's Sightless Legion — $12.95
❏ #36: The Coming of the Terror — $12.95
❏ #37: The Devil's Death-Dwarfs — $12.95

❏ #38: City of Dreadful Night — $12.95
❏ #39: Reign of the Snake Men — $12.95
❏ #40: Dictator of the Damned — $12.95
❏ #41: The Mill-Town Massacres — $12.95
❏ #42: Satan's Workshop — $12.95
❏ #43: Scourge of the Yellow Fangs — $12.95
❏ #44: The Devil's Pawnbroker — $12.95
❏ 45: Voyage of the Coffin Ship — $12.95
❏ #46: The Man Who Ruled in Hell — $13.95
❏ *NEW:* #47: Slaves of the Black Monarch — $13.95

THE WESTERN RAIDER

❏ #1: Guns of the Damned — $13.95
❏ #2: The Hawk Rides Back from Death — $13.95
❏ #3: Gun-Call for the Lost Legion — $13.95
❏ #4: The Law of Silver Trent — $13.95
❏ *NEW:* #5: The Gun-Prayer of Silver Trent — $13.95

G-8 AND HIS BATTLE ACES

❏ #1: The Bat Staffel — $13.95

CAPTAIN SATAN

❏ #1: The Mask of the Damned — $13.95
❏ #2: Parole for the Dead — $13.95
❏ #3: The Dead Man Express — $13.95
❏ #4: A Ghost Rides the Dawn — $13.95
❏ #5: The Ambassador From Hell — $13.95

DR. YEN SIN

❏ #1: Mystery of the Dragon's Shadow — $12.95
❏ #2: Mystery of the Golden Skull — $12.95
❏ #3: Mystery of the Singing Mummies — $12.95

CAPTAIN ZERO

❏ #1: City of Deadly Sleep — $13.95
❏ #2: The Mark of Zero! — $13.95
❏ #3: The Golden Murder Syndicate — $13.95

www.ingramcontent.com/pod-product-compliance
Lightning Source LLC
Chambersburg PA
CBHW052138170626
46812CB00004B/1495